PRAYERS IN BATH

WALK

PRAYERS IN BATH

Luisa Perkins

Artworks by Jacqui Larsen

MORMON ARTISTS GROUP
NEW YORK 2017

MORMON ARTISTS GROUP, 457 WEST 57TH STREET, # 601
NEW YORK, NEW YORK 10019

MORMONARTISTSGROUP.COM

"Would God that all the LORD's people were prophets"
—Numbers 11:29

"And I took the little book out of the angel's hand, and ate it up; and it was in my mouth sweet as honey: and as soon as I had eaten it, my belly was bitter."
—Revelation 10:10

For Annette

CONTENTS

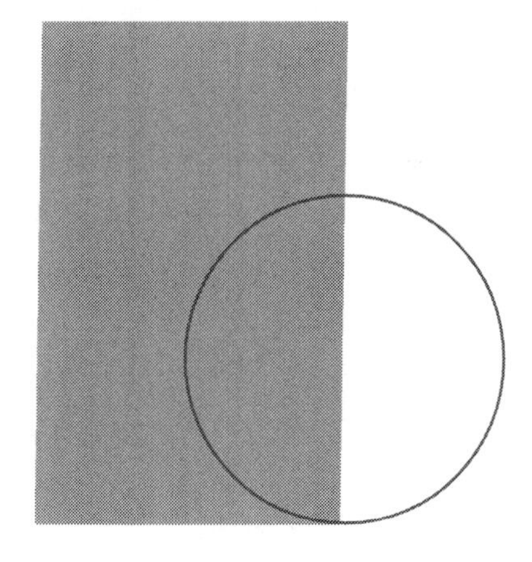

ulia leans her forehead against the bus window; its cold glass is a balm to her throbbing skin. She bites the inside of her cheek and gazes out at the gray, rainy street. Failure rests like lead in her gut.

Bath's railway station comes into view. The garish light of the sign refracts in the raindrops running down the window. The station whispers a temptation of escape. If Julia were to act quickly, she could get off this bus, which lumbers toward the flat she and Ted have been renting. She could run inside the station, holding her coat over her head against the deluge, and buy a ticket for London or Edinburgh...or even Paris or Milan. Somewhere far away and anonymous. Any place but back to the flat that isn't home.

Julia's hand rises, seemingly on its own, toward the bell pull that signals the driver to stop. But she hesitates, and the train station slides behind her into the gloom that is England at a November four o'clock. She sighs. The bus lurches on.

At the Summerhill stop, a girl levers her body out of a seat a few rows up, then waddles to the front door of the bus. Her belly is huge. One year for Christmas when Julia was little, Santa brought her a giant rubber ball with a horse's head on it. She and her brother bounced on it blissfully around the house for weeks. This girl's baby bump looks at least as big as that cheery red Hippity-Hop, maybe because the girl is otherwise so thin.

As she goes down the steps to the door, the girl catches Julia staring and glares back, rings of thick black eyeliner slightly running. Once on the wet concrete under the bus shelter, she pulls a pack of cigarettes out of her coat pocket and lights up. Bile rises in Julia's throat, and she shuts her eyes. The bus shudders back into gear and sways up the street.

Once they're on Lansdown Road, Julia has one more chance to be brave. Or to be a coward, depending on how she parses the situation. She can stay on the bus and pass right by Kingswood School where Ted works, and their drab semi-detached across the way. At the racetrack, she can transfer to another bus, one bound for Bristol. From there she can take a ferry to Cardiff. And then? Walk into the wilds of Wales and lose herself.

Instead, she pulls the bell cord and gets off the bus into the downpour. In the short run to her building, she gets drenched. The icy rain numbs her skin, but it can't quite reach her heart. After climbing the two flights of stairs to the door of their attic flat, she stands there for a minute, bracing herself. She's just about to unlock the door when it opens suddenly. She and Ted both flinch when they see each other.

"I heard you on the landing." Ted looks at the key ring clutched in Julia's hand. "When you didn't come in, I assumed you'd forgotten your keys." He pushes his baby-fine brown hair out of his eyes, a gesture as familiar to her as breathing. Stepping away from the door he says, "I take it your appointment didn't go well." His voice is rough with hope that's about to die.

Julia turns away and takes off her sodden raincoat. She gulps back a sob, clattering the hangers in the coat closet to muffle the sound. She should probably hang her coat in the bathtub, but who cares? Let it drip on the muddle of shoes at the bottom of the closet. It doesn't matter. Nothing matters anymore.

How to respond to Ted? False cheer? Resignation? Rage? There was a time when she wouldn't have self-edited for Ted. Seven years ago, when they got married, they'd lie awake late at night, sharing their hearts in the darkness. How many disappointments ago had she turned into this careful, calculating introvert?

Hands descend on her shoulders, rubbing the stubborn knots of tension just above her collarbone. She wants to shrug away so she won't soften and break down, but that would hurt Ted's feelings.

"Talk to me?" he murmurs.

Get it over with, she tells herself. She turns and looks up to stare him in the eyes. "Implantation failed again." Her words are clipped, brisk, efficient. Conveyors of information.

Ted's face falls, his hair cascading over his forehead again. Then he gives her the tight-lipped smile usually reserved for slow bank tellers and mouthy students. "So. That's it."

"That's it," she repeats.

She can almost hear a steel door slamming shut on an era of their life. Two years of being careful while they finished their degrees—hah. They had precious little money back then, and she now begrudges every dollar spent on contraception. After finishing their doctorates, spending three years on enthusiastic and creative "trying" on their own. Then twenty-four months of fertility treatment in the States and another six months here in England.

What a waste. Nothing to show for it except an empty savings account. Well, and countless bruises from all the hormone injections and blood draws. Those are slow to fade.

Ted puts his arms around her. Julia wills herself to lean into his embrace, to release the rigidity keeping her erect and letting her hold on to a shred of pride.

"I'm sorry," she whispers into his chest. That simple admission breaks her dam of self-control. Yet another failure; yet another betrayal.

Julia knows she's an ugly crier, so she keeps her face buried in Ted's sweater until she can get hold of herself again. Once the sobs pass, she breaks away and walks into the living room. The rain pounds their roof in ceaseless waves and susurrations.

Ted follows. "Are you hungry? I made some peppermint tea, and I can get out some cookies."

Of course; it's teatime. Looking at her husband, Julia tries to smile. Of course this disappointment is as big for Ted as it is for her. But it's her body, her fault. Behind his sympathy and concern, does he blame her? Does he resent her? Does he regret not marrying someone else, someone fertile?

"No thanks. Maybe later. I think I'll just go lie down for now."

"Any chance you want to have a prayer together?"

Resentment knifes through Julia, but she pushes it away. She remembers the Spencer W. Kimball quote that she's heard a thousand times, something about most needing to pray when you least feel like it. Her mouth twists at the irony. She must really need to pray right now.

And she knows it'll make Ted feel better if she agrees. She sinks down on the couch, hoping that giving in will help soften her angry heart. "Yeah, sure. But you'll have to say it."

Ted comes around the other side of the couch and kneels at her feet. She exhales and joins him on the rug. He takes her hand and begins.

After seven years of hearing it at least once a day, Ted's conversational prayer style still astounds Julia. No breathy or overly deep church voice; that's not how he was raised. Instead, it sounds as if he's talking on the phone—an easy, almost casual tone, as he makes statements and asks questions, pausing to listen for responses. Early on, his way of praying cemented Julia's love for him; someone on such close terms with God would certainly be an ideal partner for the eternities.

Now, though, as he pours out his broken heart, he doesn't leave much space for anything God might want to say back. That's fine; her will and the Father's haven't aligned this time, and she has a hard time caring about that.

After a few minutes, Ted's flood of sorrow lessens, and his

monologue transforms into his usual give-and-take rhythm. Julia shifts from knee to knee restlessly and echoes his "Amen" when he's done.

Before she can rise, Ted's arms enfold her. "It'll be okay." His breath is warm on her scalp. "There's a reason we're going through this trial; I know it."

Julia grits back a cynical reply and waits patiently. Finally, he lets go. She escapes into the bedroom, where she can wrap herself in self-pity.

She sits on the edge of their bed, which is tucked under the eaves of the tiny room. A gust of wind rattles the old windows in their casements. She stares at the framed portrait of herself and Ted that sits on her night stand. They're smiling, snuggled together, the unyielding granite of the temple behind them. She turns the picture face down.

Ted's voice comes from the living room, faint and muffled. He has likely called his parents or one of his brothers to give them the bad news. They'll probably call all of the temples on the Wasatch Front to put Ted and Julia's names on the prayer rolls. Again.

If she were truthful, she'd admit to envying Ted his insular, optimistic family. Unlike Julia, Ted was raised in the Church; he's one of those Taylors that goes back to John. His parents still live in the same house in the Salt Lake Avenues where Ted grew up; he and his five siblings went to West High, then to the U, of course taking time off from college to serve missions, every single one of them.

Ted broke the Taylor mold a bit by leaving Utah for graduate school at Berkeley, and then rebelled a bit more by marrying a convert. His and Julia's lack of children sets them even further apart from the rest of the family, who are apparently busy raising an army of Helaman.

All those nieces and nephews. Now she's crying again. She lies down and puts a pillow over her head. Breathing deeply and willing her sobs to abate, she remembers the blessing Ted gave her before this last cycle of IVF. "You will bring forth a miracle," he'd said, his voice breaking, before closing in the name of Christ. After opening their eyes, they'd stared at each other, sure that Ted's words had come straight from heaven. Julia had rushed to her journal to transcribe every word she could remember. Revelation was precious, and she wanted to show the Lord she treasured it.

She'd pored over that blessing countless times over the past few weeks, each time savoring the sense memory of the joyous spirit that had filled her whole being with effervescent warmth. This time, they'd have success. In a year, likely less, she'd hold a baby in her arms. Now her mouth twists in disdain. Where, exactly, is her miracle?

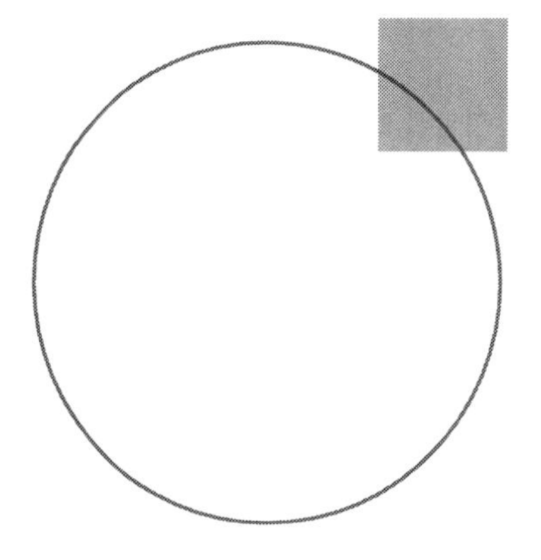

ays later, the sound of the front door shutting and Ted's footsteps in the living room shake Julia out of a doze. She bolts upright, thrashes through the bedcovers, and gropes for the clock. 3:30 in the afternoon. When Ted left for work nine hours earlier, Julia was exactly where she is now.

Ted opens the door and pokes his head in, smiling. "Hey."

"Hey." Her cheeks go hot with shame. "I...I was just about to take a shower," she lies. "I didn't realize it was so late."

She hasn't left the apartment in days. Ted has done the shopping, the cooking, and the laundry—all after his long school days, while grading papers far into the nights. There must be a limit to his patience, but Julia hasn't seen it yet.

Ted sits next to her, seeming not to notice her oily hair or stale pajamas. He takes her hand and studies the carpet for a few moments. Just when Julia is about to ask if he's all right, he takes a deep breath and says, "I have a surprise for you."

Julia pastes on what she hopes is an eager smile. "Wow, nice. How about if I shower and you make us some tea first? I'd feel more worthy of a surprise if I got myself together."

"Okay." He hops off the bed.

Once he leaves the bedroom, Julia scrambles out of bed and gets moving. Slug. Loser. Ted is soldiering on through his hurt. Why can't she?

After a quick shower, she brushes her teeth and pulls her hair into a ponytail that drips lankly down her back. She puts on a bit of eyeliner and a spritz of perfume. Squinting into the foggy mirror, she tells herself she looks presentable.

In the kitchen, Ted has made big mugs of tea—peppermint for him, verbena for her—and has gotten out some of the fancy, chocolate-covered digestive biscuits they usually save for family home evening treats. Julia's stomach rumbles. She hasn't eaten since last night, and her body is finally awake enough to complain.

She sits and inhales the hot vapor rising from her mug, then breaks off a bite of biscuit and chews it slowly. "So," she says after swallowing, "What's the surprise?"

"I hope you're not mad." Ted's eyes are shining. "I found you a job."

Julia just stares.

"Well, not a job, exactly. An internship. It's not paid, but it'll give you something to do."

"Something to do," Julia echoes.

Ted rushes on enthusiastically. "It sounds fascinating, actually. I wish *I* could take a break to work on it. They're starting a new archaeological dig at the Roman baths."

There it is. Julia now has a hook for her strong impulse to crush this ridiculous idea. "Seriously? I don't know anything about archaeology. I'm a linguist. What possible use would I be on a dig?"

"You don't have to know anything. It's more of a dogsbody-type situation. Two archaeologists are heading up the particulars. They have some graduate students on board, but they need a few people to help with the dirty—"

Julia gets up from the table. Stuffing the rest of the biscuit in her mouth and chewing furiously, she goes to the window and stares down at the concrete courtyard. An old broom and a broken tricycle cast long shadows in the fading light. She should be out there with the rest of the useless trash.

Trash that doesn't want to be a happy worker bee in some hole in the English mud. Trash that doesn't feel like being patronized. Julia grips her upper arms and forces down her rising rage. Ted just wants to help. She turns around. Ted stares into his mug, his biscuits untouched. She sits back down, but when he speaks, he doesn't look up.

"I'm trying, Julia—really. I'm so worried about you. I guess I would grasp at anything if it would help. I'm sorry." Ted sips his tea and goes on. "Chamberlin's cousin is one of the lead archaeologists, and when Chamberlin mentioned the part-time gig today at lunch, it sounded like the perfect thing to get you out of... the house a bit. But I can call the cousin back and tell her that it won't work out after all."

Ted's humility is an arrow to the heart of Julia's indignation.

She sighs and eats another biscuit. Then she puts her hand on his and wills him to meet her gaze. "When does it start?"

Ted looks at her. His shine is back. "You'll do it?"

"Sure. Why not. We're here for the rest of the school year at least, right? I may as well make myself useful."

On Sunday, Julia would prefer to stay home from church, but she's promised to accompany Brother Davies for a special musical number, and she can't let him down. He's been a diligent and kind home teacher, and she finds his raspy baritone voice as comforting as a trusty old blanket.

In sacrament meeting, after the youth speaker sits down, Julia and Brother Davies go up to the stand for their performance.

During practices, Brother Davies's interpretation of "Guide Us, O Thou Great Jehovah" was pleasant, but today, he puts something extra into his singing. He sings the first and second verses in English.

We are weak, but Thou art able; hold us with Thy powerful hand...

The peace that swells within her feels as though she's being lowered into a perfectly hot bath. Julia feels the ice around her heart start to melt. She presses her lips together as she plays, but tears well up anyway, and at the end of the second verse, she has to dash them away quickly to see the music. With a showy interlude, she changes keys, and then Brother Davies comes in again, now singing in his native tongue.

He chews through the Welsh consonants with relish and

vigor. Though Julia's ears take in only crusty, rich syllables, her heart hears a clear message. It comes to her unbidden; her mind was on the music and holding herself together. But now she knows: this archaeology internship is exactly what Heavenly Father wants her to do.

A cloud of light enfolds her, even though there is no change in the chapel's literal illumination. The internship is not merely a random kindness. This is God's plan for her. She is in Bath at this time, for this work.

Brother Davies finishes, and Julia's last chord follows. She fears she might float off the piano bench. As she rises unsteadily to her feet and walks back to the pew where Ted sits, the light and buoyancy fade. The calm assurance does not. For the first time in days, the future doesn't appear drab and colorless. Ted puts his arm around her as she sits, and to her surprise, she finds herself snuggling into his side in response.

Julia has walked up the Kingston Parade before, but now two beige modular buildings have been erected against one honey-colored wall of the ancient abbey. The smaller modular is merely a shed but has a large, shiny combination keypad on its metal door. The other building is where she is supposed to meet Professor Alice Thayne, the cousin of Ted's boss. Julia mounts the aluminum steps and knocks on the cheap, hollow door. A sturdy-looking woman in brown tweed opens the door wide.

"Mrs. Taylor?" The woman's tea-stained teeth do not diminish the brightness of her smile.

"Yes." Julia enters. "You must be Professor Thayne."

"Yes!" the professor takes Julia's hand and pumps it enthusiastically. "Thank you for coming to meet with us. We're anxious to get to know you. Come, have a seat." The professor walks to a square, Formica-topped table, where a man who could be Colin Firth's better-looking younger brother rises from his seat. "This is Professor Martin Fletcher, my co-chair on this project."

When Professor Fletcher shakes Julia's hand, he holds on to it for a fraction of a second too long. Confused, she meets his eyes, and he raises one eyebrow at her. Is he flirting? Julia instantly dislikes him. Trying to maintain a polite face, she pulls away and goes through her backpack to find her resume. Handing it to Thayne, she says, "I have absolutely no experience at this kind of thing, you'll see."

The professor scans the sheet of bond paper. "Experience is not necessary. I do need to file this with our sponsors, but they've left the hiring particulars to us. And I have a good feeling about you. Someone who can complete a Ph.D. with honors in linguistics at Berkeley can surely think on her feet, follow protocols, and make good decisions, yes?"

"Yes." Julia smiles.

Fletcher clears his throat. "In which area of linguistics is your speciality?"

"The Romance languages. I wrote my dissertation on the dialects of Romansh spoken in southeastern Switzerland."

"How fascinating," Thayne says at the same time that Fletcher murmurs, "How obscure."

Julia glances at Fletcher, shocked at his rudeness. His sculpted face is perfectly neutral. Maybe she's imagining it, but he seems to be baiting her somehow.

Thayne says, "So your Latin must be good."

"It's quite solid, actually."

Thayne looks at Fletcher and grins. "There now, Martin. I told you. Of course she's overqualified, but her skills may come in handy. You never know what we'll find."

"What do you mean?" Julia asks.

"There have been settlements at Bath for millennia. The allure of the hot springs must have been even greater before the advent of modern plumbing and power. In AD 43, the Romans came to England and annexed the Britons. They co-opted Sulis, the local Celtic goddess, to keep the peace." Thayne points to a photograph on the wall, which shows an old, weather-worn statue. "They saw Sulis as a manifestation of Minerva, which I'm sure is no surprise. Many of the relics found here during previous excavations have had Latin inscriptions on them." Thayne laughs. "But I'll stop myself before I get any further into lecture mode. If you want to know more about what we're doing, I'll give you a copy of the grant proposal. It outlines all of the history in great detail. We need to do a quick background check on you—finger-stick DNA test, fingerprints—but it's just a formality. When can you start?"

Julia is surprised at how quickly things are moving. "How about tomorrow?"

Thayne looks at Fletcher, who nods. She extends her hand

to Julia again. "Brilliant. Be here at 9 o'clock, if you can. Welcome aboard."

CHAPTER TWO

wo weeks later, Julia has taken Professor Thayne up on her offer and has read through the detailed—and successful—grant proposal. The archaeology team has a specific and finite plan for sifting through the debris that has silted up the Roman drain leading from Bath's hot springs to the River Avon. The project will have the side benefit of clearing the drain for better flow, so the City of Bath has kicked in additional resources. The time allotted to Thayne's team is apparently much less than for a usual dig; the powers that be at the Abbey has contracted to have radiant heating installed under the entirety of the church's ancient stone floor soon, and the archaeologists must be out of the way before that work begins in a few short weeks.

Previous digs in Bath have recovered several jewels and other personal items belonging to the ancient inhabitants, but this project will go deeper than any earlier excavation. In the weeks since they began, the team has diverted the normal flow of the hot spring down another channel. Fans run day and night to pull moisture from the remaining meter-thick clay.

The Roman builders arched and lined the sewer so meticulously that in two millennia, the stones have shifted little. The structure is in better shape than buildings hundreds of years younger. Sulphur from the hot springs has leached into the ancient boards lining the sewer's floor and now oozes up from the clay. The pervasive odor of old eggs and bad cheese made Julia gag when she first started the internship a fortnight ago, but she's getting to the point where she doesn't notice it as much—a fact that makes her nervous. What if she's soaking up the smell at the dig, then emanating it when she emerges, offending everyone around her? She makes a mental note to beg Ted to clue her in if she starts to reek.

Julia hasn't seen much of Thayne or Fletcher since their first meeting. She mainly interacts with Bronwen Jones, a graduate student who oversees the grunt work. Bronwen has shown Julia how to use the various sieve-like screens, instructing her to scoop the damp clay then coax it through the layers of mesh, which get progressively finer with each frame.

She kneels on the kind of rubberized foam cushion one takes to sporting events. The huge work lights on their mantis-like stands keep the worst of the chill away, but she's still wrapped in Ted's old ski jacket, a watch cap, and two scarves her mother knitted for her years ago. It all clashes, but Julia doesn't care. Her fingerless leather gloves are a cheap pair bought at the local gardening store, but she was right not to invest in something more expensive. These gloves are already impregnated so deeply with clay that even though she scrubs and rinses them every evening, they stiffen into exoskeletons by morning.

Julia sets aside anything she finds that won't go through the screens, bagging each anonymous fragment and labeling it with a code that denotes exactly which cubic meter of the vast, echoing drain it came from. At the end of the day, she puts all the bags in an orange plastic bin, which she labels with the same code, then turns it all over to Bronwen. Where the bins and bags go after that, Julia doesn't know. Maybe the archaeologists will share the next step of the process with her at some point—but if not, that's fine, too. For now, she is content.

The job is both tedious and demanding of attention, and Julia's perfectionism turns out to be an asset. Once in a while, she stops to wonder what she's sieved. A tooth? A wood chip? A kidney stone? A fossilized seed? She has no way of knowing, since she's under strict instructions not to clean the items she finds. That work is reserved for the professionals, Bronwen has told her solemnly.

Despite the dank air, monotony, and darkness, Julia has come to love the work. It's a twenty-minute walk from their flat, which is a comfortable distance even in late November. Bronwen and the other interns keep to themselves, and the fact that they have never struck up a personal conversation with her endears them to Julia. At her station in the dig, she is alone with her thoughts and her gritty cuticles and her set of screens and her never-ending buckets of silt. She feels herself starting to heal, beginning to come to terms with a new definition of herself as a non-mother in Zion. At least for now, she has a purpose other than being Ted's wife.

Julia's stomach tells her it's almost time for lunch. As usual, she's brought a thermos of hot verbena tea, a roast-beef sandwich, some chocolate-covered malt balls called Maltesers, and a rosy Cox's Orange Pippin apple, a variety that's dense and juicy and sweet-tart. Delighted to debunk the English stereotype of heavy, inedible meals, Julia has found the food in Bath to be wonderful. Especially the meat and produce—fresh and flavorful, often from a nearby farm or county. Her mouth waters at the thought of her apple. She pulls back the cuff of her glove to check the time. Almost noon; she'll sieve one more bucket before taking a break.

This area is nearly done. She goes through another bucket of dirt carefully, but finds almost nothing this time. That's not unusual; some loads of silt have lots of chunks, some don't. She bags and labels the bits she does find, then sets the screens to the side of the dig so she'll remember where to start again after lunch.

As she moves to the stepladder, Julia stumbles over something sticking up between the sewer's widely spaced floorboards. She has excavated that area as directed, but something hard juts up slightly from the compacted surface. Since it's between floorboards, it's technically outside her area of responsibility. But whatever it is, Julia wants to move it so she won't trip over it again. She takes an orange plastic putty knife out of her pocket, squats down, and delicately levers around the object. Probably a rock—but maybe not.

Easing the object out of the clay takes several minutes, and holding it up to the light, she can see that it definitely is not a rock. She brushes away as much mud as possible, revealing a cylinder about the size of a can of tomato paste. It's far heavier than it looks, though, and definitely not a can. Julia's heart beats faster, and she takes in a deep breath to call out to Bronwen.

But then she stops. The light she sensed two Sundays ago while playing for Brother Davies returns, swirling within her and warming her chilled nose and fingertips.

Don't show it to Bronwen or the others. Don't show it to anyone. Hide it.

Despite herself, despite knowing that no one else is in this part of the tunnel, Julia looks around. The voice in her mind is so clear, so definite.

Hide it. The voice is more insistent this time.

Julia doesn't wait to be told again. She stuffs the cylinder, mud and all, into the pocket of Ted's ski jacket. After filling in and smoothing over the new divot in the sewer's floor, she climbs out of the trench, grabs her backpack, and heads for the surface.

The modular where she first met Thayne and Fletcher serves as the team's breakroom. A key Bronwen gave Julia hangs on a lanyard around her neck, along with a photo ID that allows her access to the dig site. As usual, Julia finds the modular empty; she likes to eat lunch around noon, while everyone else prefers to break for elevenses and again at tea time. The door locks behind her automatically, but today, Julia turns the deadbolt.

She sets her backpack, scarves, and hat on the Formica table and goes to the sink, where she takes off her gloves and scrubs her hands. The warm water helps thaw her fingers further. Glancing at the door, she takes the cylinder out of her pocket and rinses it off. She takes care to make sure all the grit goes down the drain, then dries off the object with a paper towel and holds it up to the fluorescent light.

The doorknob jiggles, and then the deadbolt clicks. Julia shoves the cylinder into her pocket just as the door opens. Her heart thuds faster and harder than the feet of a clog dancer. Professor Thayne comes in, along with a gust of wind, and shuts the door against the cold.

"It's monkeys out," she says breathlessly, unwinding a very long scarf from her neck.

Julia takes a step back. Her coat pocket suddenly feels ten times heavier than it did before.

Professor Thayne comes forward after shrugging her parka into a plastic chair. "I'm guessing from the look on your face that you have no idea what I just said." She grins. "No matter. How are you liking the project? Bronwen tells me your work has been excellent."

Julia pictures what's in her pocket and tries to smile.

"Well, we're glad to have you," Thayne continues. "I'm sure we'll be seeing more of each other. That is, if you don't get too bored and decide you've had enough of us." Professor Thayne pulls a box of PG Tips teabags out of a cupboard and fills the electric kettle. "Could you do with a cup?"

"No, thank you." Julia gestures to her backpack. "I've got my own."

"Lovely! Let's sit for a minute then. You're on lunch, yes? I didn't get breakfast this morning, and I'm famished."

Julia would rather leave so she can eat her lunch and look at the object in peace, but she can't think of a graceful exit. She swallows and nods. As the professor makes tea and microwaves a Styrofoam box, Julia removes her jacket and hangs it on a hook near the door. She piles her scarves on top to hide sagging in the side pocket, then sits at a chair facing the coat hooks so Thayne will have her back to it. Anxiety radiates from Julia, but hopefully she looks normal. She takes her lunch out of her backpack, unwraps her sandwich, and sets it on a napkin.

Finally, the professor sits down with her mug of tea and a paper plate filled with curry-smelling something. "Ah, that smells good. My tum's been a bit dodgy lately, but I finally have my appetite back." She digs into her lunch. "So!" Thayne says after a few bites. "Tell me more about yourself. I'm not admitting anything, but pretend I've forgotten everything my cousin told me about you and your husband."

To gain a few seconds and gather her thoughts, Julia bites into her sandwich and chews it thoroughly. "My husband Ted is writing a biography of Jane Austen, so we're here for research for the next several months. He teaches Fifth Form American Literature classes at Kingswood School to pay the bills. I..." She takes another bite. She won't be mentioning the real reason she's currently jobless. "The school didn't need a French or Latin instructor, and other than that, I'm not terribly employable."

Professor Thayne smiles and bobs her head while forking curry and rice into her mouth. "Well, you're in with the right crowd, then. We're all overeducated and underemployed. Thank

God for the Western Power grant funding this dig, or the whole lot of us would be slaving as cashiers at Sainsbury's." She chuckles at her own joke and wipes her mouth. "Seriously, though, we're very grateful for your help. I wish we could afford to pay our interns."

"Not necessary. I've actually enjoyed it."

"Lucky us."

They eat in silence for a few minutes, and then Thayne tells a funny story about her destructive but adorable Irish setter. Julia laughs at all the proper moments, but rushes through her food so she can leave as soon as possible. All she can think about is the cylinder and what it could possibly be—and knowing that if Professor Thayne learned of it, she'd be fired, possibly even arrested.

Calm down, Julia, she reminds herself. She gathers her lunch detritus and stands.

"Well, I'm going to duck into the Abbey gift shop for a minute before my break is over," Julia says. "It was nice seeing you again, Professor. Thanks again for giving me something to do."

"It is I who must thank you. Cheers for the chat. I'm sure I'll see you soon."

"Yes. Bye."

Julia bundles herself up, keeping the pocket with the cylinder facing the door. She'll hide in the gift shop bathroom and give the cylinder a quick look, then get back to work and pray that the hours until her shift are over pass quickly so she can go home and examine her find at length. She waves at the professor before shutting the door of the modular and hurries across the street to the gift shop.

BRING ME MY ARROWS

ocked in a stall of the gift shop bathroom, Julia takes the artifact out. The outer bathroom door crashes open; she hurriedly shoves it back in her pocket

For a panicked moment, Julia's convinced it's a police raid. The thought makes her break out in a cold sweat. She'll get carted off to jail for stealing from the dig. She closes her eyes and tries to moisten her cottony mouth. But then the soft slap of sneakers on the tile and the squeaky wheels of a stroller tell her she's safe.

"Mum! I need to wee *now*!"

"Please hold it just a second longer, Jasper. Let Mummy get your trousers undone." Rustles, zips, and snaps come from the next stall.

Julia lets herself out and goes to the sink. As she washes her hands, she looks at the reflection of the scene behind her.

The woman, crouching on the tile floor, hasn't closed her stall. She's helping a little fair-haired boy balance on the toilet seat. He looks about three years old, and his bright blue eyes catch Julia watching. She flinches, focuses on rinsing away the soap, and turns off the taps.

She's drying her hands and about to make a quick exit when the toilet flushes. The boy runs out of the stall, pants around his ankles.

"Honestly, Jasper!" His mother tries to look stern, but ends up laughing. She catches her son and deftly snaps and zips him back up, despite his best wiggly efforts to escape. She picks him up and moves to the sink. She glances at Julia and grins. "Kids. Can't live with 'em, can't sell 'em."

Julia forces a laugh, then goes out quickly before the woman notices the tears in her eyes. Outside, she leans against the wall to get herself together. Is this how it will be forever—every child she sees a knife in the heart? She has to find a way to get over this and get on with her life.

But at the moment, Julia needs to get back to work—after she finds a better hiding place than her sagging pocket. She looks through the jetsam in her backpack and comes up with a stretchy mitten that has lost its mate. After looking around to make sure she's alone, she puts the cylinder inside it. She shoves the mitten to the very bottom of her backpack, then piles petrified tissues, old receipts, and candy wrappers on top of it. Ted has always rolled his eyes at Julia's messiness, but today, the chaos in her backpack serves her well.

Back at her work station in the sewer, Julia resumes sifting and screening. She can't relax into her habitual lull, though; all she can think about is the cylinder and the odd but unmistakable command she obeyed to hide it. A current of anxiety underlies her thoughts, making her as jittery as if she'd mainlined Dr. Pepper.

"Mrs. Taylor?"

Julia can't quite stifle a small yelp. She turns toward Professor Fletcher, who stands above her trench. From below, he looks even taller.

"I do apologize for startling you." A leer disfigures his handsome face. "But I'm delighted you find the work so absorbing."

Is her heart beating as loudly as it seems? Does she look anxious? She widens her eyes and tries to smooth any stress out of her expression. "Hi, Professor."

Fletcher rocks back and forth on the soles of his leather-bottomed shoes. "Good afternoon." His formal greeting sounds like a correction. "I wondered whether you might be able to assist me for a few moments. My Latin's a bit rusty, and I've got an inscribed piece I'd like you to evaluate."

"Oh. Okay, sure." Her voice is squeaky; she clears her throat. "Where is it?"

"In the museum lab. Can you join me up top?"

"Right now?"

"If that's convenient."

Julia feels uneasy, but can't think of a polite way to refuse. Besides, why would she turn down an opportunity to contribute something more significant to the project than sieving through kilo after kilo of clay?

"Of course, Professor." Julia stacks her screens and removes her carapace-like gloves. She snatches her backpack, not wanting it out of her sight. As she moves to climb out of the trench, Fletcher holds out a hand to her. Again, she can't refuse without looking rude. His sweaty palm is slick against the grit on her skin, and once she's out of the trench, she resists the urge to wipe her hand on the leg of her jeans.

"After you." He indicates the way out with a slight bow. His manners are perfectly gentlemanly; why does that seem so creepy?

Fletcher leads the way up the spiral staircase to the surface and out of the shed that protects the entrance to the sewer. They pass the break-room modular and go to a side door of the bathhouse, which now serves as a museum. They wend their way through the museum's crowded main hall, down a back hallway, and to a door marked "Employees Only." He raises his eyebrows in his annoying, overly familiar way as he swipes his keycard, and then holds the door open for her.

She ducks into the cavernous room, veering as far from his outstretched arm as possible. She stops a few steps into the room and looks around. It's an impressive sight: several well-equipped worktables, a bank of state-of-the-art computers, and a large-format digital camera. This project is well funded, indeed. Unfortunately, no one else is in the lab at the moment. Julia would rather not be alone with Fletcher, but can't think of any way around it. And she's probably overreacting. Isn't she?

Now she sees the destination of the bags and bins she's

been filling. They're neatly stacked in rows against one wall, across from the largest worktable, which is surrounded by long-necked, full-spectrum lights. The contents of a dig bag lie on its surface, some items clean and tagged, others still covered with dried-on clay. Under a large, lighted magnifier sits a metal bottle. It's about the size of an egg, but with a flat bottom and a throated opening like a trumpet's bell.

Fletcher hands Julia a pair of latex gloves and puts on a pair himself. Then he flips on the ring of lights surrounding the magnifying glass and bends over to inspect the object. Despite her wariness, Julia is curious. Still peering at whatever it is, Fletcher motions her closer.

"I believe it's an unguentarium, something one would expect to find at a public bath. Indeed, past digs have recovered several. Later, we'll do an analysis of the inside to determine what exactly it once contained, but the inscription is what caught my attention. The letters go around the edge of the flask's mouth." He moves aside with another one of his creepy little bows. "Have a look and see what you think."

Julia goes to the magnifier, sets her backpack securely between her ankles, and looks through the glass. Fletcher is right; tiny letters are spaced evenly around the thin lip of metal. "May I touch it?"

"Be my guest." Fletcher moves closer to her and leans forward as she gloves up and then rotates the little bottle between her thumb and forefinger. His breath wafts over her shoulder, strongly minty, but with cigarette smoke and the faintest hint of rot beneath. Julia suppresses a shudder and focuses on the flask.

"*Modest—tina...*" She reads slowly. "That's likely a woman's name, or possibly the name of a village? But the last four letters—V, H, E, E—don't spell a Latin word. Maybe they're initials."

"But see here," Fletcher puts his hand on the small of Julia's back and leans in even farther. Julia stiffens and grits her teeth. He puts his hand over her fingers and turns the flask, his shoulder lingering against hers. "I thought it might be V, A, L, E, 'vale,' as in 'Modestina, farewell,'" he murmurs. "Maybe it was a parting gift, either to or from someone named Modestina. Which would be rather romantic, don't you think?"

Julia has broken out into a sweat. She sets down the flask, coughs into the crook of her elbow, and edges away from him. He doesn't look at her as his hand falls away casually back to his side. He's still looking at the flask through the magnifier, appearing completely absorbed—but his neck above his shirt collar is flushed.

"I...don't think it's 'vale,'" she says. How can she make a quick but graceful exit? "I can see how the H could be an A, but that third letter is definitely an E, not an L." She backs up another step. "Maybe you could email me a digital photograph of it. I could enlarge it and study it later tonight after dinner. With my husband."

She looks at her watch. It's only 2:45. "In fact, he's expecting me to meet him at Kingswood School in a few minutes," Julia lies. "I should probably get going."

"Of course." Fletcher finally looks from the magnifier up at her, his face neutral. "Do what you like. I shouldn't expect an unpaid intern would feel as dedicated to this project as I am. After all, this is my life's work." He draws himself up and looks down his perfect nose at her. "Thank you for your time, Mrs. Taylor. You've been most helpful." His cold voice belies the statement. He bends over the worktable again.

She's been dismissed. "Happy to help anytime," she says, voice a little too cheery, and hurries out.

Despite the relief in getting away from him, Julia feels snubbed. Which is ridiculous, since Fletcher is repulsive in the extreme. She should feel nothing but gratitude for an excuse to get out of here. What if he hadn't been rebuffed so easily? She shudders again as she strips off the latex gloves and tosses them in a trash bin.

Once outside the museum, she squints up at the pale blue sky. What now? She can't go back to the dig, or Fletcher will catch her in a lie. But then she realizes that he's handed her a couple of extra hours to study the cylinder. She texts Bronwen a quick apology for leaving early, even though she won't get it until she returns to the surface. To Julia's surprise, a reply bounces back almost immediately.

No problem. I've gone home early as well. Stomach virus or food poisoning: not sure which. See you tomorrow. I hope.

Poor Bronwen; what rotten luck. With her supervisor down for the count, all Julia's hesitance about leaving early flees. Winding her scarves around her neck, she walks quickly against the sharp wind up the old stone streets.

Julia and Ted usually have Family Home Evenings on Tuesdays, since Kingswood's library is open late on Mondays and Thursdays, and Ted can do research there right after school until late into the evening. Ted's there now, so after Julia arrives home, she has hours to scrutinize the cylinder. The light is best in the kitchen. She sits at the table and turns the artifact over in her hands. It's about four inches long, an inch and a half in diameter, and looks like it's made of lead. Has anyone touched it in centuries? The workmanship is fine, and it's definitely not modern—to her inexperienced eyes, it looks as old as Fletcher's unguentarium.

She peers at its smooth edges. The cylinder is not solid, she sees now; there's an even crack around one end. It has a lid. She shakes it gently, but hears nothing. It's so heavy, though; if it is a container of some kind, it can't be empty. Does she dare open it?

She's come this far. Chest warm, blood pumping, she sets her fingernails under the raised edge of one end and pulls. Nothing. She tries again, grunting with effort until she's afraid her nails will break. The lid doesn't budge. Maybe it's sealed or soldered shut. She could use a butter knife to try to pry it open...but lead is too soft for that, isn't it? She can't risk leaving a mark on it.

She remembers the gloves Fletcher gave her, and winces. She shouldn't even be touching this with her bare hands. Stupid. This whole thing is probably stupid on a criminal level, but Julia feels compelled to keep trying.

After wrapping the cylinder in a dish towel, she hides it in the bottom kitchen drawer under a bunch of mismatched plasticware lids. She grabs her purse and runs down to the corner pharmacy for a box of latex gloves. She grabs a packet of chocolate biscuits, too, hoping the sugar will calm her nerves. Back in the flat once again, she checks the time. Still good. Ted won't be home for a while yet.

With gloves on, she tries opening the cylinder again, and this time the lid budges the tiniest bit. Maybe it's the extra traction provided by the latex; maybe the metal has finally warmed to room temperature and expanded slightly. She adjusts her grip and tries again, and the lid comes off so suddenly that Julia cracks her elbow on the back of the chair.

Her eyes water at the pain, but she wipes the tears away with the crook of her now numb elbow and looks inside the cylinder.

Spiraled tightly inside are some sort of thin metal sheets. They're not lead, like the cylinder; they have more of a coppery gleam. She turns the cylinder over and jiggles it gently. The scrolled sheets drop into her palm, just like that.

Julia's breath catches in her throat. Tiny writing covers the surface of the metal. The characters look familiar, but she can't quite place them.

Footsteps on the landing outside startle her so badly that she almost drops the scroll. If it's Ted, he's home much earlier than usual. Quickly, Julia puts the scroll back in the cylinder and wraps it up again in the dishtowel. She hears a key turning in the front door lock: Ted. By the time he enters the kitchen, she has hidden the cylinder and the gloves in the same junky bottom drawer and is putting away the clean dishes from breakfast. She does her best to keep her breathing calm as Ted kisses her cheek.

Then he sniffs. "It smells funny in here."

"Yeah?" Julia hasn't noticed any odor, but then she remembers how her nose has stopped registering the rotten egg funk of the sewer. She keeps her head down as she sorts silverware into the drawer. She's sure her face is as red as it feels.

"Yeah, it smells like the chain-link fence at my grandpa's house after it rains. I like it, actually. Brings back good memories. But random, right?"

Julia gestures at the half-open window. "Maybe it's something in the courtyard. I guess it rained earlier, no surprise there."

"That must be it." Ted flops onto a kitchen chair, still in his jacket. "Man, I'm hungry. For some reason, I couldn't concentrate on my writing tonight, so I thought I'd come home instead of banging my head against my carrel. How about if we get a bit of dinner and then walk down to the Bath Museum? It's open late on Mondays. We've both been working pretty hard. We deserve a treat."

Julia's heart no longer feels ready to leap out of her chest. As desperate as she is to look at the scroll more closely, she can't do it with Ted here. She purses her lips at the irony of having been behind closed doors at the museum just hours before. But it's true that she hasn't seen any of the actual exhibits yet. "Sure. I'll just get my coat."

They have steak and kidney pie at the pub up the road, sharing a large piece of sticky toffee pudding for dessert. Afterward, bundled against the November wind, Ted takes Julia's arm in his and pulls her close.

"Are you sure you want to walk all the way into town?" Julia asks.

"Why not? You do it every day. The air feels good. And I've realized lately that we haven't done enough exploring. Before we know it, our time here will be up. I don't want us to look back with any regrets. Besides, after that meal?" Ted pats his trim gut. "I could use the exercise to help me digest it. Unless you're too tired."

"No, my stomach is a little unsettled, but I'm all right."

Ted stops in his tracks. "You don't think..."

Grief rises up in Julia, sharp and hot. She forces it down with irritation. Every hint of indigestion for the past five years has been a hopeful sign of the nausea that comes with pregnancy. "No, I *don't* think. It's not possible, remember? Dinner was really rich. The walk will do me good."

Ted ducks his head as if he's been reprimanded. "All right, if you're sure."

They walk in silence for a few blocks. Julia thinks about her hidden treasure. She's already nervously questioning her actions, which is surely why dinner isn't sitting well. But if she's not going to be open with Ted about what she's found, she can at least go along with what he'd like to do. And she should ask him about his work, anyway.

"How's Jane this week?"

"She's good, mostly. I'm hoping to incorporate more of her correspondence into my draft, but that may mean heading to Oxford one of these weekends if I don't want to rely only on what's been digitized so far." Ted goes on for a bit about the weaknesses of previous Austen biographies, and Julia is happy to listen.

At the museum, Ted shows his teacher ID, which gets them in free. They pick up a map and wander around. It's a well-thought out exhibition space, and Julia realizes that Ted's right: they really should take advantage of being here. Someday, when they're back in the States, their time in England will be a distant memory. She wants it to be a good one.

"Hey, look." Ted points to a shaded area on the map. "An exhibit of artifacts from past digs. Maybe it'll inspire you. Who knows what the team might find this time?"

Alarm shoots through Julia at his question, but she follows Ted into the dim, tasteful exhibition room, where specially lit glass boxes hold fragments of brittle metal.

Julia leans close to decipher the oxidized writing on one of them. It's in Latin: *Deum Mercurium, ut nec ante sanitatem...* She glances at the explanatory plaque on the side of the display.

"What's it say?" Ted asks.

"It's some sort of curse. Whoever wrote it had his donkey stolen, and he's asking Mercury to curse the thief with bad health until he returns it."

"Wow. Okay."

They move to the next box. These are all curse tablets, the plaque explains, written by patrons of the baths and thrown into the hot springs. Most are offerings to the goddess Minerva Sulis, but a few are addressed to Mercury as well. Julia translates them for Ted as they walk along the perimeter of the room. Most of them call for justice regarding things stolen at the baths, but a few are prayers for a lover or a sick child.

At the last box, Julia stops, her eyes widening. This curse tablet is not in Latin. These characters are exactly like those on the scroll hidden in her kitchen drawer. The characters are Brittonic, she reads, and this tablet is the only existing example of the language.

If that's true, why did the writing on the scroll look so familiar to her earlier? Both do resemble Nordic runes; perhaps that's it.

She reads on, wondering whether there's any connection between her scroll and these bits of metal. The tablets here are far more degraded, certainly—maybe because they weren't sealed in lead cylinders.

Brittonic. She racks her brain. Her memory of Celtic languages is hazy at best. She needs time to prowl around on the

Internet. But this is a huge deal. The scroll she has is written in this language; she's more sure of it by the second. She's burning to get home and examine the scroll in detail.

She looks up. Ted is still standing next to her, not looking at the curse tablet, but smiling at her instead.

"How long have you been watching me?" she asks, feeling obscurely guilty.

"Brittonic, eh?" He gestures to the plaque. "I love seeing you wrapped up in a puzzle. I haven't seen you look this alive in months."

"You know how much I love linguistics," she says. "This is a language no one knows anything about." She is about to say more, but stops herself before she gives away her secret. She bends over the glass again.

Ted puts a hand on her shoulder. "I'm sorry, honey. About all of this. We came to England for me. When I'm done with the research for this book, it's your turn. If you want to move to Switzerland or the south of France to do fieldwork or something, let's do it. I can write anyplace. We can take turns forever, and live anywhere we want."

He's so sweet and unselfish. She knows many men who wouldn't make that kind of offer, wouldn't regard their wives' careers as important as their own.

"Deal," she says, straightening up and grinning. "I'll have to come back to this exhibit another day, maybe after work. I'm sure you're ready to move on, but I could stay here for hours. This all fascinates me."

"I had a feeling it would," he says.

“What do you mean?” Her words come out a bit sharper than she had intended.

“I’ve been praying for you. As I do every day, of course, but this afternoon, I had a feeling that I should bring you to this museum, that it would perk you up.”

Julia’s smile returns. Sweet man. “And it has. Absolutely. Thanks.”

They walk home, and Julia feels both closer to Ted and further away from him. She doesn’t want to hide anything from him, but life is pretty black and white for the Taylors. Ted’s a rule follower, whereas she’s always been a bit more of a rebel. Iron rod vs. Liahona. She’s not sure he’d understand why she took the scroll from the dig, and she doesn’t want to risk ruining the mood between them by telling him about it right now.

For the first time in a while, things seem...normal. Tomorrow, she’ll figure out what to do with the scroll—maybe put it back, pretend to rediscover it, and hand it off to Bronwen or Professor Thayne.

She feels faintly uneasy at that idea, but puts it out of her mind for now. She needs be in the moment and pay attention to Ted; he always gives his best to her, and he deserves her best in return.

he next morning, after Ted goes to work, Julia calls Bronwen to say she's not well.

"I think I'm coming down with a cold," she lies.

"Not a stomach thing? Lucky bird." Bronwen snorts. "I'm better today, but last night was bloody awful. I must be a half a stone lighter, which is the silver lining. The sewer is no place for you, though, not with all the damp. Stay home and drink lots of tea with honey."

Julia thanks her and hangs up.

After bolting the front door, she puts on gloves and takes the cylinder out again and sits with it at the table. Today it's sunny, rare weather for late November, and light fills the flat. Carefully, Julia eases the scroll out of its casing. She touches the edge of one of the coppery pages, terrified that it will be as brittle as the curse tablets at the museum. But this metal is flexible and shows no sign of oxidation. Holding her breath, she peels back the first of the thin sheets. Bright and distinct, paragraphs of words march down the page, as orderly as if they'd been typed.

These are definitely the same kind of groupings of letters as she saw on the Brittonic tablet the night before. Though she's studied only Latin-based languages in depth, linguistics is, above all, a discipline of recognizing patterns. As she scans the writing, she notes one word that appears over and over.

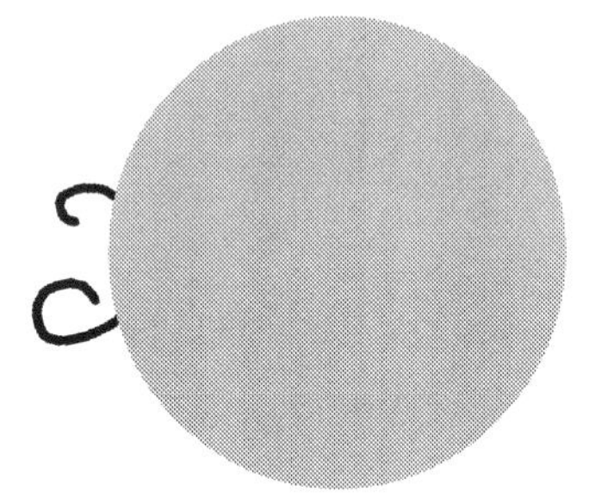

She sets down the scroll. She knows this word; the realization brings a lump to her throat.

"Jesus."

She whispers it to herself like a prayer, feeling as if she'd plunged into one of the hot springs. Now the other runes begin to make sense. Pushing back her chair so quickly that it skids across the linoleum, she grabs the message pad and pen from their spot near the phone, sits down again and transcribes what she is reading. *Because she understands what she is reading.*

Slowly at first, working her way outward from each instance of the name of the Savior, the words resolve themselves in her mind and become clear. She writes them down and covers page after page, soon writing as fast as she can and shaking out the ache in her fingers and wrist every few minutes.

Sentences and paragraphs spin themselves into vivid movie scenes in her mind: the resurrected Christ healing, teaching, praying, smiling. Multitudes around him pressing close to touch him, embrace him, ask him questions. His patient responses, the way he treats each person as if he or she were the only one present. A calm, healing heat spreads from her chest throughout her whole body. She has never felt healthier, happier, more alive, more alert. She wants this feeling to go on forever.

Her phone rings. Julia jumps a mile. She answers it, gasping from the shock. "Hello?"

"It's Bronwen. I'm sorry; did you run for the phone? I hope I didn't wake you."

"No, no! Not at all." Julia looks at the clock. It's past noon. Where have the past three hours gone? "I...was just in the bathroom. How are you? Is everything okay?"

"Oh yes, of course. I'm on my break and thought you might need some Lemsip or cough sweets. Can I stop by the druggist and bring you anything?"

"How kind of you." Remembering her lie, Julia fakes a cough. "No, I think I have everything I need, but thank you so much. I'm sure I'll be back at the dig tomorrow."

"All right, well, rest up. Professor Thayne sends her best."

"Thanks, Bronwen. See you soon."

Julia hangs up. She's horrified at her subterfuge. But she looks at the scroll again, and exhilaration soon pushes out the guilt.

Now, though, she needs to put away her treasure. She wraps the pages back into their original spiraled form, and is relieved to see that they show no signs of having been disturbed—no creasing or wear. She should have thought of those things before, but no matter. She closes the cylinder and wraps it in the cloth, but now she should find a more secure hiding place. She doesn't want it found; she doesn't want it damaged. There aren't many options.

She walks around the flat. The old fireplace is sealed shut. Their small shared bedroom closet is full to bursting. In the bathroom though, she finds the perfect spot. Under the sink, a little door in the wall opens to the plumbing. There's just enough space for her to wedge the cloth-wrapped cylinder between pipes. She shuts the door and sits back on her heels with satisfaction. Ted should never have a reason to look there.

Back in the kitchen, she looks over the pages covered with her writing—about half of the little notebook. She carefully rips the pages out of their binding, then takes them to the bedroom and gets out her laptop. Transcribing takes a lot less time than translating by hand; Julia is a fast typist. In another hour, she's entered everything and saved it in an encrypted file, which she copies onto a thumb drive. She slips it into her jewelry box, and then changes her laptop password.

Despite her right hand, which is throbbing with the unaccustomed strain of so much writing, she yearns to pull the scroll out again and translate more. She's aghast at how time has flown by without her knowledge, however. It could happen again, this time with Ted coming home and surprising her. She'd better wait. She sits down with a neglected basket of laundry and starts folding clothes.

Tell Ted.

The calm, clear words are as unmistakable as ever, but she shakes her head and keeps folding. She's not ready for Ted to hear this. What she's done will shock him; Ted's never stolen a pen or even a paper clip. A priceless artifact that will probably be on the UNESCO World Heritage list at some point? The enormity of it hits her all over again. No. He's not ready. She's not ready.

Tell Ted.

Not yet, she answers back. *I want to keep it quiet a bit longer.* And, she admits, she wants to translate it all first, before Ted makes her give the scroll back. Which, of course, he would. And she can't chance that.

Merely thinking of the possibility makes her stomach go sour. What exactly has she gotten herself into? Images of prison, crushing fines, and infamy flash through her mind.

But flashes of horror along these lines don't last for long. Fear can't replace the magnitude of what she's found, and she grins despite herself.

Her stomach rumbles, and Julia remembers she hasn't eaten all day. She decides to run to the market and get a sandwich along with the regular shopping. She grabs her coat and purse and gets halfway down the stairs when she remembers the notepad pages, still lying in a shuffle on their bed. She runs back for them and shoves them in the pocket of her jeans. Then, at the bus stop, she rips them into tiny shreds and sprinkles them into the public garbage bin. Evidence disposed of.

After dinner, the phone rings again. Ted's washing the pasta pot in their toy-sized kitchen sink, so Julia takes the call in the living room. She goes back to the doorway once she hangs up.

"That was Brother Davies," she tells Ted above the clatter and splash. "He and his wife want to have us over on Thursday for an American Thanksgiving dinner. The bishop and his wife will be there, and they've invited another American couple who just moved here from New York. I told him I thought we could make it. Can you skip the library that night?"

"I forgot it was Thanksgiving week," Ted says with a smile. "Sure. It's a holiday, after all, even if it seems a little awkward to celebrate it in the U.K. Thoughtful on their part, isn't it? Did he ask us to bring anything?"

"When I asked, he requested a pie. I'll do my best, but I'm betting Sainsbury's doesn't carry canned pumpkin. I could manage an apple tart, I think." Julia takes a towel out and starts drying the dishes.

"Great," Ted says. "Maybe you could stop by the farmers' market tomorrow after school and look for some cider. We could take that along as well. Or some chestnuts, maybe."

"Good idea. I have no idea what the Welsh idea of an American Thanksgiving dinner in Somerset will be like, but whatever it is, I'm sure it'll be nice."

The next morning at the dig, the tedium of the work chafes

instead of soothes. All Julia can think about is the scroll and wanting to finish her translation. The minutes crawl by. At the stroke of noon, she puts away her gear and goes down the tunnel to where Bronwen is working.

"I'm pretty tired," Julia says. "I think I'll call it a day."

"Oh, of course." Bronwen pushes her curly hair out of her eyes, leaving a smear of clay on her forehead. "You probably shouldn't have come back to work today. You should only work half days the rest of the week. You don't want anything to settle in your lungs."

Half days: that's perfect. With a straight face, Julia says, "I hate to say it, but you're probably right. As long as you think that's okay."

"I probably shouldn't tell you this, but you get twice as much done as any other intern I've ever supervised. We'll be able to stay on schedule. Go home and rest. And have some more Lemsip!"

Julia smiles and remembers to walk away slowly. *You're sick,* she reminds herself.

Once she's above ground, she decides she'll eat her lunch at home, and walks briskly up Lansdown Road.

Back in her kitchen, after gulping down some food and cleaning up the kitchen, she gets out the scroll and some blank paper from the printer. This time, she sets the timer on her phone so she won't be caught unawares again.

She finishes late in the afternoon, thirty-seven minutes before the timer is set to go off. Translation and transcription are complete; the work has gone much faster this time. She sits back, staring at the laptop screen, and breathes as quickly as if she just climbed a hill. Her mind feels so alive and electric that she wouldn't be surprised if her hair were all standing on end.

As before, she backs up the file and rips up her handwritten notes, this time going to the kitchen and slipping the shreds under some wet garbage in the bin. She'd better get going on the apple tart.

As she mixes up the crust and peels and slices apples, she hums to herself, pondering the enormity of what she's discovered and what she's done with it. After the tart is out of the oven, bubbling, golden, and fragrant, her satisfaction increases.

At dinner, Ted puts his hand on hers on the scarred wooden table until she looks up from her plate. "I can't tell you how happy it makes me to see you back."

"What do you mean, 'back'?"

"You're your old self. I caught a glimpse of it at the museum the other night, but I haven't seen you this happy since you were writing your dissertation. I guess it was a gradual thing; I didn't realize how worn down you'd gotten by all the disappointment. All this trying for a baby...I know it's been harder on you than it has been on me, and I'm really sorry about that. But now, it seems like you're moving on a bit, and I think that's good for us both."

His blue eyes, so assured and kind. She loves this man; she can trust him. "Ted..."

She opens her mouth to tell him about the scroll, to share the most amazing thing that's ever happened to her. But fear holds her back once again. "...I love you," she finishes, but Ted doesn't notice how lamely she's trailed off.

He squeezes her hand and grins, then pulls her up out of her chair. "I love you, too. Come on," he murmurs.

She follows him into their room, and for the first time in a couple of days, she forgets all about the scroll.

SHINE FORTH

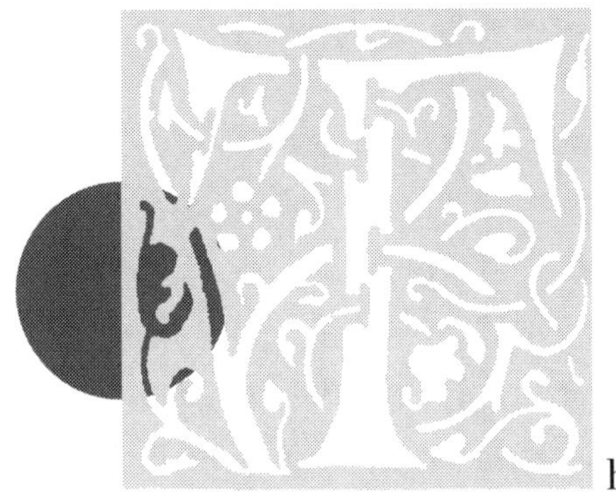

hanksgiving Day, Julia hurries home after her morning at the dig. She stops by the farmers' market and strikes out when it comes to cider, but does find some chestnuts. In the flat, she tosses her coat and bags in a pile on the couch. She'll tidy up later. Ted is meeting her at the Davieses' at 6:30, and she has a lot she wants to do before then. She spends the afternoon online looking up scriptures, all the while making notes in her journal. Third Nephi, The Gospel of Matthew: the more she reads, the more excited she gets. Everything she's translated fits perfectly into what she knows of Christ's post-resurrection visits.

"Other sheep I have, which are not of this fold..." Why wouldn't some sheep be in England, too? Or in Africa or China, for that matter? She imagines other records hidden around the world; how many more might there be?

Getting ready for dinner, she smiles at herself in the bathroom mirror. She's wearing a cranberry-colored sweater that Ted loves. He was right about her looking different, she realizes. She glows with health and energy. Her hair even seems to have a bit more bounce and body, though that may just be because her hormones are getting back to normal after all the fertility treatments. But it does seem as if finding and translating the scroll has brought her back to life, in a way.

Tonight, once they're home from dinner, she promises her reflection, she'll tell Ted everything. He'll be shocked, but he'll understand when he realizes the enormity of what she's found. Of course he will, and he'll help her figure out what to do next. Because, what, exactly, is she supposed to do with this discovery? She hasn't thought into the future at all.

But this much she's already worked out: Tomorrow morning, she'll put the cylinder back where she found it, buried in mud between the floorboards. She'll track down Professor Thayne and show it to her so that she can excavate it. Julia will choose her moment carefully; she doesn't want there to be any chance that Fletcher will get his treacherous hands on it. The scroll and its contents are too sacred for that.

Wearing her good coat, she carries the wrapped-up tart to the front door, but at the last moment, runs back into the flat for the chestnuts.

Brother and Sister Davies live a couple of miles away; she'd walk if she weren't carrying so much food. Under the bus shelter, Julia takes a long sniff of the late autumn air. Rain, wood smoke, fallen leaves: even if she's thousands of miles from home, it smells like Thanksgiving should. She smiles again.

With hugs, Brother and Sister Davies welcome her inside their cozy house, and they take her offerings with enthusiasm.

"Your husband just arrived," Sister Davies says as they walk into the living room.

It's a snug spot, filled with comfortable old furniture. Framed etchings and old maps hang on the walls, and the shelves on either side of the fireplace are double stacked with books of all kinds. A spinet sits in the corner, its top covered with tidy piles of music.

Ted stands at the hearth, warming his hands at the picture-perfect fire. He doesn't turn around. After handing her coat to Brother Davies, Julia goes to Ted's side, leans up, and kisses his cheek. He stares at the flames and doesn't even give her his impatient fake smile. "Hi, honey," he says, his tone perfectly civil—far from the easy warmth he usually greets her with.

What's wrong? Flustered, Julia turns back to their hosts and scrambles to cover her confusion and embarrassment. "Uh... Sister Davies, is there anything I can do to help with dinner?"

Their hostess is looking at Ted with a furrowed brow, but she nods at Julia's question. "Everything is ready, dear, but come on in the dining room. Bishop and Sister Wells are picking up the Memmotts. They should be here any minute. Ye can get the water glasses filled while we wait."

Why won't Ted look at her? Has he gotten bad news from his publisher? Has something gone wrong at school? If either were the case, he would have probably texted or called her. It must be something else. She'll have to find a way to get him alone for a second before dinner begins.

Sister Davies has decorated the dining room table with bunches of oak leaves and acorns. The red and gold are striking against the snowy linen. As she fills the water glasses, the doorbell rings. Julia hears Brother Davies's cheery greetings and introductions. Everyone crowds into the small room, Brother Davies and Ted trailing behind a couple that must be the new Americans. Bishop Wells introduces them.

"Steve and Sheila Memmott, you met Ted a moment ago. This is Julia, his wife—and here's Sister Davies."

Julia smiles and nods politely, not letting her face fall at the sight of Sheila's protruding belly. The Memmotts look very young—they can't be older than 23 or so. How nice for them.

"Take your seats, everyone," Brother Davies directs. Julia's place card is between Bishop Wells's and Steve Memmott's. Ted sits across the table next to Sister Davies. He still won't meet her eyes.

"Will you offer the prayer, bishop?" asks Brother Davies.

Everyone bows their heads.

The bishop asks a blessing on the food and the house. As always, Julia is charmed; to her, all prayers somehow sound truer and more official when they're offered in an English accent. After the chorus of amens, Sister Davies jumps up and starts bringing food to the table. Everyone admires the roasted goose, which Brother Davies carves.

"I couldn't get a turkey, I'm afraid," says Sister Davies. "My apologies to the Yanks. This probably isn't the most authentic

Thanksgiving meal."

"It looks wonderful," Ted says. "I've always wanted to try goose. It's so Dickensian."

Nothing about the meal is anything Julia's ever encountered at Thanksgiving Dinner before—except for the mashed potatoes and gravy—but it's all delicious. She ends up only picking at her food, though, because her gut roils with anxiety. Throughout the evening, Ted laughs and jokes with everyone except her.

He must be angry; there's no other explanation. Has he found out about the scroll? That seems impossible, but what else could it be? Her anticipation over telling him everything has soured into dread, and she finds it difficult to concentrate on the conversations going on around her.

She does pick up the fact that Steve Memmott has come to England to work at a software company. He and Sheila have rented a house in Claverton Down, a posh suburb across town. Julia thinks of their tiny, drafty walkup flat and gets even more depressed.

At least her apple tart is a hit with everyone—except Ted asks only for a piece of Sister Wells's famous banoffee pie. The subtle dig, more than anything that's happened this evening, brings Julia to the point of tears. She stares at the candlelight glinting through her water glass and wills away the lump in her throat.

Brother Davies pushes back from the table with a contented sigh. "I hoped we could do some singing after dinner," he says. "This Sunday's the first week of Advent, so I pulled out some carols. Singing always ushers in Christmas for me. Julia, would you play for us?"

"I'd love to." Anything to make the evening go by faster. What should have been joyous has turned to ashes. Somehow, she ruined the evening for Ted, and he's ruined it for her in return.

Before singing, they all clear the table together, but Sister Davies declares that the kitchen is too small for anyone to help with dishes. "I don't know any of ye well enough to be that close to ye," she tuts. "Brother Davies and I'll tend to it later."

Julia sits at the spinet in the living room and plays a few chords. The small piano has a lovely, if quiet, tone. Brother Davies hands round the carol books, and everyone takes turns requesting favorites. Many of the English carols aren't familiar to Julia, so she sight reads, singing a soft alto after a verse or two. The eight of them make a decent choir, it turns out; Steve has a gorgeous tenor voice, and Sheila's soprano is competent.

Sister Wells suggests another carol unknown to the Americans. It has several verses, though, and by the third time through, they're all singing parts, more or less. The lyrics of one of the last verses jump out at Julia, so astonishing that she can barely keep playing:

> And at this season of the year
> Our blest Redeemer did appear,
> And here did live, and here did preach,
> and many thousands he did teach.

Here did preach? Heat pounds through Julia, and the narrative she's translated from the scroll runs through her brain in Technicolor. If she's interpreting the song correctly, here's more evidence that what she discovered is real. But how did it become public knowledge?

When they've finished the carol, Julia looks up at Sister Wells. "That's a lovely one. What does that verse mean about Christ preaching here? Is the carol supposed to be set in the Holy Land?"

"Oh, no, dear. I don't think so, anyway. I've always assumed that it refers to the Glastonbury legend."

Julia's face must look as blank as her mind feels, because Sister Wells continues. "Ye've never heard it, then? That Jesus came to England as a lad with Joseph of Arimathea, his rich uncle? Lots of folk believe it. And it's not out of the question, is it, given what Latter-day Saints know about Christ in America? If He traveled there, why not here?"

Brother Davies chimes in. "The legend's as common as salt all over Britain. Surely you've heard 'Jerusalem.' It's England's unofficial anthem."

Julia shakes her head, but Ted says, "My students sing it at chapel every Friday. It has a nice melody, but I guess I haven't paid attention to the words."

Sister Davies goes to a rosewood cabinet and rifles through the music inside. "We have an arrangement of it—four parts, a cappella. It's not a Christmas carol, but it's as English as Yorkshire pudding." She hands out the music. "Julia, can you play it through? And then we can all try it. Most of the time, the tune is sung in unison, so everyone will have to work a bit."

The lump in her throat bigger than ever, Julia plays through it once, reading the lyrics along with the notes.

And did those feet in ancient times
Walk upon England's mountains green
And was the Holy Lamb of God
On England's pleasant pastures seen?

"This is it," Julia whispers. What she's translated is real. The story on the scroll...it all fits. She tries to be subtle about wiping her eyes.

Brother Davies conducts them as they sing, but Julia can barely voice her part. After they've sung through both verses, the bishop puts his hand on Julia's shoulder. "Beautiful, isn't it? Though it's very nationalistic—maybe not appropriate to be sung at an American Thanksgiving party." He smiles at his own joke, obviously trying to lighten her mood, but of course, he has no idea why tears are streaming down her face.

She's not about to clue him in, either. She glances at Ted, whose face is grim. Oh. For just a few moments, she'd forgotten his mood. She needs to get him home and find out what's wrong, whatever it is.

"It's gorgeous." She sniffs and then fishes in her pocket for a tissue. "Sister Davies, may I borrow this copy until Sunday? And..." She hesitates, looking at her watch. "Speaking of Thanksgiving, this has been an absolutely wonderful evening, but it's getting late. In the States, tomorrow is a holiday, but I know that's not true for any of us, is it? We'd better go."

Steve looks at his phone and agrees; Sheila sags against him a bit, her hand resting on the significant shelf of her belly. She looks as if she'd be grateful to get to bed as soon as possible.

They take their leave with warm goodbyes all around, and after the Memmotts drive off with the bishop and his wife, Ted and Julia walk to the bus stop through the misty night.

"What's wrong?" Julia asks, the minute they're out of earshot. "I know you're upset with me. What's going on? What happened?"

The bus arrives just then—a minor miracle, given the late hour.

"Let's talk at home," Ted says, still not looking at her.

They sit in silence as the bus bumps down the road. Julia is in more turmoil than ever, and she fears she might lose the small amount of dinner she managed to eat. Has she caught Bronwen's stomach bug? She clamps down on the nausea, determined not to make a scene and upset Ted even further. Patience, she tells herself. Whatever it is, they'll work it out. She holds on to that thought tightly.

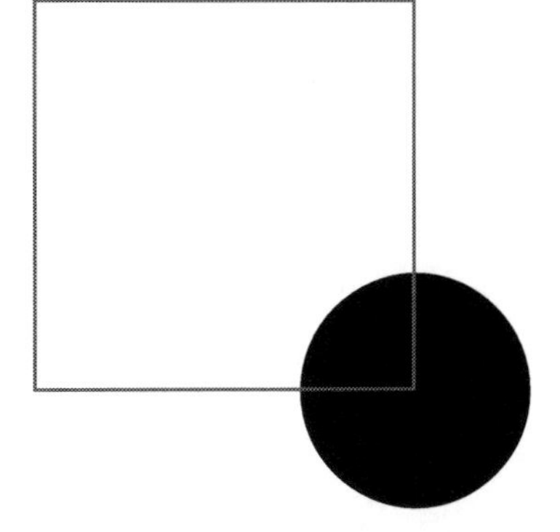

Ted turns on Julia in the kitchen once she's put the leftover tart in the refrigerator. "Where were you today? You weren't at work."

"I was there in the morning...wait, how do you know I wasn't at work?"

"That doesn't matter. Where have you been?" Ted spits each word as if it tastes bitter.

"I was here, at home."

"You were here. In our flat." His mouth twists on the sarcasm.

Julia hurries to explain. "I called in sick."

"But you weren't sick. Why would you lie? And why wouldn't you tell me you were staying home?"

Now's the time for Julia to tell him everything, but this is not how she wanted it to be. No joy or wonder; only anger and fear. She's disgusted with herself not following her initial prompting to confide in him days ago. In Ted's current mood, he won't be receptive to the scroll or the translation she's made.

Ted's staring at her, the muscles in his jaw working. Too late, she realizes that her silence looks like she's trying to come up with an excuse. "Ted, I—"

Ted cuts her off with an upraised hand. He takes a deep breath. Then, "Are you having an affair with Martin Fletcher?" he chokes out. Pain disfigures his face.

Julia remembers Fletcher's hand on her back as she looked at his unguentarium in the lab and shudders. "Not if he were the last man on earth. How disgusting." But Ted's accusing eyes make her angry and defensive. "Seriously? Absolutely not. How could you *think* such a thing? An affair? Why is sex the first place your mind went when you found out I wasn't at work? I've never given you any cause to distrust me or to suspect that I would ever even think of another man. How *dare* you?"

Ted turns away and rubs his face vigorously. "Sure, get mad at me. The best defense is a good offense, I guess."

She grabs his shoulder. "No, Ted, really. Why would you think that?"

He shrugs her hand off. "Alice Thayne met Chamberlin for lunch today. I ran into them in the school parking lot, and Professor Thayne mentioned that you'd been out ill. I tried to cover up the fact that I had no idea what she was talking about, but I'm sure I looked like an idiot. You know what a bad liar I am. Can you imagine how embarrassed I was? So I drove over to the abbey and found Fletcher in the modular. When I asked whether he'd seen you, he laughed and made all kinds of insinuations about the two of you. I had to leave before I decked him."

Ted trembles; Julia sits down in shock. Fletcher has been even more traitorous than she could have imagined.

"So I'll ask you again," says Ted, pushing his hair off his sweaty forehead. "What's going on between you two?"

"Nothing!" Julia is reeling. "Absolutely nothing, though not for lack of trying on his part. He's repulsive. I've already told you that. Why would you believe him instead of me? And how could you think I would do such a thing to you, to us?"

Ted drops to his knees on the linoleum and takes Julia's hands. "Then where have you been? Why would you skip work without telling me?"

Julia stares into her husband's eyes. She banks on the likelihood that having taken the scroll will not be anywhere near as bad as adultery. How best to start the story of what she's done—with show, or tell?

Words aren't enough, she decides. She squeezes his hands and stands up. "I'll be right back."

She heads to the bathroom, pulls the cylinder out of its hiding place, and goes back to the kitchen. She sits in her usual chair, fully aware that she's stalling. Ted is still kneeling on the floor. "Maybe take a seat?"

He does as she asks, all of his attention on the bundle in Julia's hands. She unwraps the cylinder and sets it on the table, then gets the box of gloves from the back of the cupboard under the kitchen sink. She hands a pair to Ted, then opens the cylinder, which is now much easier to do than it was the first time. She gently tips the scroll out into her palm, fans its shining pages slightly, hands it to Ted, and waits.

"I assume you found this. At the dig." It's not a question. He still won't look at her.

"Yes." Now, with the truth out, she knows how he must see her: Irresponsible. Untrustworthy. Dishonest.

"You stole it." His voice is barely audible.

"I…no! I didn't steal it. I just…borrowed it. I'm putting it back tomorrow, I promise. That's been my plan all along."

He sets the scroll on the table as if it carries plague germs. "But why? Why would you take anything you found? Besides the fact that it's plain wrong, I can't imagine any greater sin on an archaeological dig. What were you thinking? You signed a contract. Thayne and Fletcher will definitely press charges against you for ethical violations. The authorities could put you in jail, or fine you thousands of pounds, or kick us out of the country, or all three. And the scandal would follow us; you can bet on that. No one will ever hire either one of us again. You had to know that. Why would you take such a risk?"

Julia closes her eyes. Ted's right; her behavior makes no sense on the face of it.

He's never going to believe me, she tells the Lord silently.

Just try, comes the answer, along with a trickle of peace and calm.

She tries to dismiss the whisper, then remembers that this whole situation has come to pass because she didn't listen last time. *Okay*. "I felt prompted to take it."

Ted's laugh is almost a sneer. "You felt *prompted* to break the law and violate the terms of the internship agreement." His voice gets louder. "You felt prompted to lie to your coworkers and to me. I hate to tell you this, honey, but that's not how the Holy Ghost works. People don't get promptings to do stupid, foolhardy, unethical, illegal things." He's yelling now; Julia can't remember him ever raising his voice at her.

"Ted, please listen. I took it because I felt that I should."

Ted rolls his eyes.

"No, I really did. It was a command. I know that sounds bizarre. But it was like Nephi, you know, when he was commanded to kill Laban?" Julia swallows and hopes for a response. Ted doesn't acknowledge her reasoning, but she keeps going. "And when I got it home and opened it, I realized I could translate it—and I felt as if I had to. I *wanted* to. *That's* what I've been doing with my afternoons, here, in our flat. *Not* sleeping around with that revolting bully."

Ted picks the scroll back up and fans its pages delicately, scanning the runes. "You translated it." His voice is flat, uninflected.

"Yeah, I did. Here, hold on. I'll show you." With a bit of hope, Julia runs to their bedroom, grabs her laptop, and hurries back, opening and powering it up on the way. She enters in the password to the file. "I'm really excited about this. It's amazing. I can't wait for you to read it."

She sets the computer on the table in front of Ted and takes the scroll from him. Carefully, she puts it back in its cylinder and closes it. After putting it safely in her sweater pocket, she sits and watches him reading. His eyes track back and forth across the screen. After a few minutes—which feel like an eternity—he scrolls to the next page, and then the next. He's not reading anymore, merely scanning. His face looks like stone.

Doesn't he see? Is he not recognizing what the translation must be?

He scrolls faster and faster now, and when he reaches the end, he looks up, tight-lipped. He shuts the laptop a little too firmly. He gazes at Julia for a long moment, then strips off the gloves and, leaning back, tosses them into the trash from where he sits.

"Well?" she finally asks.

"Well, what?"

"What do you think?"

"I doubt you want to know." He glares at her. "But if you insist, I'm sick to my stomach. Because what I think is this: either this is all some kind of monstrous fabrication you've come up with as a prank, or you're delusional. I hope it's the latter, which would make sense, given all of the stress you've been under."

Julia feels slapped. This is her worst nightmare come true. "So, either I'm lying to you, or I'm crazy. Thanks for the show of trust, Ted."

"How could you possibly think I'd believe that this is an actual record of Jesus visiting England? You finding it and miraculously translating it contradicts everything we know about modern revelation. For one thing, you're not the prophet; he's the only one authorized to give new knowledge to the Church."

Julia stares. "Knowledge to the Church? I wasn't on planning on publishing this or anything. It's private. I felt like I should show it to you, nobody else. It's been like a gift, just for me. I know I'm not the prophet. I'm not Mosiah, and I'm certainly not Joseph Smith. Is that the only reason you doubt me?"

"No, Julia. Look. You haven't been a member of the Church all that long, relatively speaking. Ten years of membership isn't the same as growing up with the gospel, so of course there's stuff you wouldn't necessarily understand. And one of them is this—and I know how politically incorrect this sounds—but scripture doesn't come through women. Women don't write them, and they don't translate them."

Julia gets up and goes to the kitchen sink. She braces her hands against its edge and breathes heavily. She might really throw up this time. "You have never, ever played the priesthood card with me, or with anyone else, as far as I know. In every calling you've ever had, you've always stood up for women having voices at church and being valued and treated like equals. This conservatism, or chauvinism, or whatever it is—is hitting me out of nowhere, like an ambush."

She turns and looks at her husband as if he's a stranger. "Women don't translate scriptures," she repeats. "Not that we know of, right? That's what you meant. Right? Women could have written down spiritual experiences, people like Sariah or Deborah or Mary Magdalene. You've said it before yourself; that's all scripture is: a selected history of God's dealings with people. And He's talked to other people. Jesus said that Himself in Third Nephi."

Ted says nothing.

She tries again. "What about Miriam? What about Deborah? What about that verse in Joel, where it talks about daughters prophesying in the last days? Peter quotes it in Acts, chapter two. Why would he quote that, if it weren't going to come true?"

"It seems like you've built up quite a case, but this is not the order of the Church—"

Julia interrupts before he gets any more patronizing. "I'm not claiming that what I found is on par with The Book of Mormon, to 'flood the whole earth' with knowledge, or anything. I'm not Joseph Smith; I get that. But what if I was meant to find this simply because God loves me the same way He loves all His children? Am I entitled to personal revelation, or not? Does God care about me as an individual, or not?"

"This is different."

"How?"

"Honey, if you can't see how, I think we should go see Bishop Wells about this."

"The bishop? No! I haven't done anything wrong."

Ted slaps his hand on the scarred wood of the table. "Are you kidding me? If you really believe that—and I can't imagine how you can—then after we see Bishop Wells, we should see a psychiatrist." He gets up and walks out of the room.

Julia takes the cylinder out of her pocket and stares at it. The rejection she felt at the Davieses's dinner has grown a thousand times worse. She can't let this go; she has to make him understand.

She follows him to their bedroom. Ted sits in the dark on the edge of the bed. When she puts her hand on his shoulder, he twitches. "Ted, please."

"I need time." His words are clipped.

"I'm not delusional, and I didn't make this up. I've been dying to share this with you, but I was afraid. When I realized what I was reading, I couldn't believe it. Christ in England, after His Resurrection! It's a paradigm shift; I know that. But I would never set myself up as some kind of spiritual authority for others."

"It's late. I have to teach tomorrow. I can't talk about this anymore right now."

"Ted..." She lets out a breath and looks at the clock. It's almost midnight. She can't take this any further tonight; it wouldn't do any good to try. "Okay. I can sleep on the couch, if you want."

"You don't need to do that."

But he doesn't say another word or even look at her while they brush their teeth and undress. After Julia puts the scroll away under the sink, she slips into bed, conscious of Ted on his side, facing the wall, as rigid as a plank. She stares up into the darkness and listens to his breathing, knowing he's still awake. They lie like that for hours.

O CLOUDS UNFOLD

hen Julia awakens and sits up in bed, she's alone. It's after eight in the morning, so Ted's at work. Of course he is, because Ted is always where he says he's going to be. She flops back onto her pillow. Bronwen will be expecting her to show up to work soon. Can Julia make herself get up and do what she promised?

Tears leak out the corners of her eyes and drip coldly into her ears. Where is the light and warmth she felt so abundantly while translating? Will she ever feel it again? Everything is gray and dead now. The hollowness in her chest cuts through the fog in her mind.

Get up and do something.

She has to, of course. She can't lie here all day, putting off the inevitable. Groaning, she sits up and wipes her face with the sleeve of her nightgown. She kneels by the side of the bed and bows her head.

"Heavenly Father," she whispers, even though she's alone in the flat. "I'm so sorry. Please forgive me for not listening and for wanting to do things my way. Please help me to get back on track. What do You want me to do?"

She listens for a few moments, hoping for an answer. Her bare knees get sore and itchy from being pressed into the cheap carpet. She sniffs, distracted by her need for a tissue, then tries to focus again. She senses nothing, so tries a different tack with the Lord.

"I kept the truth from Ted. That's where I went wrong, isn't it? I'm so sorry. Please, help me fix this."

No words come to her mind, but she feels a wisp of the Spirit, and the tundra that is her heart softens a bit. She can make this right.

"Thank you," she murmurs. She gets up, blows her nose, and gets in the shower. While there, enveloped in the steam and heat, she reviews her plan for the morning. Photograph the pages of the scroll. Smuggle it back into the dig, then "find" it again and call Professor Thayne over to see it. After that, the whole mess will be out of her hands.

Armored in her usual layers of cold- and damp-fighting outerwear, Julia makes her way down the tunnel toward her usual workplace. The cylinder sits heavy in the pocket of the zipped-up hoodie she wears under Ted's ski jacket. She nods to Fletcher as she passes, forcing down a surge of panic. Being found out now would be an awful irony. She stops at Bronwen's station.

The graduate student smiles up from the trench where she

kneels. Her nose is already red from the chill in the air. "Feeling better?"

"Much better, thanks." Julia squints farther down the tunnel, but doesn't see anyone. She opens her mouth to ask whether Thayne is around, but then remembers that she doesn't want to draw attention to herself. "Okay, then. I'll start where I left off." She waves to Bronwen and keeps walking.

At her station, she sets up carefully, getting her screens and bags in place. After looking up and down the tunnel, she picks up a trowel and squats down. She pries some of the clay out of the wide space between two floorboards and sets it aside. She forces the ski jacket's zipper down past the place where it always sticks, and its teeth grate the edge of her hand. Wincing, she sucks on the cut for a second. This has to get done. She pulls the cylinder out of her pocket and buries it in the divot except for one edge that peeks up slightly above the planks. A scuff with her gloved hand helps hide the traces of her meddling.

She's just standing up again when a voice comes from above her.

"Mrs. Taylor."

Fletcher. Julia's heart goes into overdrive; him discovering her secret is her worst nightmare. She does her best to assume a calm expression before looking up.

"Good morning, Professor." She shifts her weight as slightly and naturally as possible, covering the top edge of the cylinder with her heel.

But Fletcher notices her movement, and his eyes narrow. "What were you doing on the floor? That's beyond your purview, isn't it?"

Sweat trickles down Julia's back. She holds up the trowel. "Just smoothing a spot I kept tripping over," she explains.

"Ah, I see." He stares at her without saying anything more.

After a silence that grows in awkwardness with every second that passes, Julia clears her throat. "Was there something you needed?"

He looks her up and down before answering. "I had a visit from your husband yesterday afternoon," he says.

Julia wishes she could slap the smirk off his face. "Yes, he told me."

"Ah, so he found you, then? I hope you hadn't gotten yourself into any sort of trouble." His tone says he hopes otherwise.

"Not at all. Just a miscommunication." Julia is sure her wide smile looks as fake as it feels. "But thank you for your...concern." She pivots toward her bags and bins while keeping her heel in place, then looks back at him.

Fletcher runs his gaze over her again, as if she were naked instead of swathed in goose down and wool. "You're quite welcome," he murmurs in what Julia is sure he believes is his most seductive voice. "I'm going up top for a smoke. Ciao."

Julia watches him until he's out of sight beyond Bronwen's station, then bends over, leaning her hands on the edge of the trench. She forces herself to breathe slowly. Now's the time to call Thayne, while Fletcher is away from the dig for a few minutes. She gives him a couple of minutes to get up to the surface, then looks down at the dull gleam of the cylinder's exposed edge. It appears, to her untrained eyes, at least, as if it has never been moved. She fills her lungs with air, then calls out, "Bronwen! Professor Thayne?"

Bronwen comes hurtling down the tunnel seconds later. "What is it? Are ye hurt?"

"No, not at all. I...I think I found something." Julia beckons Bronwen into the trench. She jumps down beside Julia.

"Where? What is it?"

Julia points. "It's outside of my area, and I didn't know what to do."

Bronwen takes a brush out of her back pocket and sweeps away some of the clay Julia has just put in place. She sweeps faster as the surface is revealed. "Wow." She sits back on her heels and squints up at Julia. "Do me a favor? Run go get the camera at my station. I don't want to go any further until I've documented every step of this process."

Guilt surges through Julia; she replaced the cylinder close to where she found it, but it's by no means exact. But she obeys. She returns with the camera, and Bronwen takes it almost without looking at her.

"Go get Professor Thayne. This might be a big deal. She needs to take over from here."

"Right." Julia hurries down the tunnel to where the professor has been working lately, but she's not there. Julia travels the length of the dig, but the professor is nowhere to be found. She runs back.

"I can't find her," she announces breathlessly to Bronwen.

"Rubbish." Bronwen looks at her watch. "I forgot. She's at a press conference. You'd better get Fletcher instead."

"But..." She can't make a scene. Involving Fletcher is the logical next choice. He's the dig's second in command. The request is reasonable. Julia fights back a wave of dismay.

"But what, Julia?" Bronwen pushes her hair out of her eyes, leaving a smear of clay on her forehead. "Please go get him! We can't just stand around here. I saw him go up top a few minutes ago."

"Of course. I'm sorry."

As she hurries up the tunnel and climbs the ladder to the surface, Julia reminds herself that the cylinder doesn't belong to her. The idea of Fletcher touching it and exploring its mysteries galls her, but that's just pride.

Fletcher stands just outside the shed that protects the dig entrance, sheltering his lit cigarette from the brisk wind.

"Professor Fletcher, could you come down? There's...something you should see. Bronwen sent me to get you."

Without a word, he stubs out his cigarette, then pushes past her into the shed and down the ladder.

Julia takes in the fresh, cold air and tries to shake the tension from her shoulders. She can't go back down yet. She doesn't want to watch Fletcher take possession of her treasure—and she's afraid she'll somehow betray herself either to him or to Bronwen. Instead, she walks down the Kingston Parade and turns toward the River Avon. The wind pushes at her back, and a drove of dry leaves clatters and sifts along the sidewalk before her.

For the few short days she had the scroll, she felt fully alive, as if the beating of her heart were the pulse of the universe. Her hope and sense of purpose had been similar to how she felt on the few occasions she'd briefly been pregnant—before her body shut down and rejected the new life within it.

But this time, she shed her purpose voluntarily; she relinquished the scroll, and she has no idea what, if anything, she'll do with the translation. Maybe nothing at all. Her marriage is her first priority, isn't it?

Isn't that what she believes? That her marriage is more important than anything outside her personal salvation? That's what Ted has always said, quoting apostles and prophets.

Does he still think that? She feels as though having hidden her discovery from him is a minor thing in the grand scheme of their relationship, but Ted seems to feel differently. She hopes he'll at least be willing to talk about it once he's had some time. She tries to imagine life without him. She'd be a hollowed-out husk. They have become a part of each other.

Passing under the tasteful maroon awning of a coffee shop, she glances through the rippling glass of the old paned windows and goes inside. She scans the scrawled-over blackboard behind the counter, a paean to caffeine: coffee upon coffee, tea after tea. Is there anything she can order?

"A large hot chocolate, please," she asks when it's her turn. "With whipped cream and cinnamon."

She reaches for her backpack and realizes it isn't on her shoulder; it's at her station in the sewer, along with her phone and her wallet. She feels her face flush as the cashier narrows his eyes at her. She rummages through various layers of clothing. Fortunately, a five-pound note turns up in the inside pocket of Ted's jacket.

"Keep the change," she says as she hands it over, her relief making her magnanimous.

She takes her mug to an empty chair by the window. The rickety table before her has one uneven leg, and it tips and bumps when she tries to use it. Giving up, she sits back and lets the hot, glossy ceramic warm her stiff fingers.

Do Bronwen and Fletcher wonder where she is? Have they called Professor Thayne about the scroll yet? Do they suspect anything? Will Julia be in trouble after all? Something a college roommate used to say pops into her head: *What are they going to do, fire me?* She stifles a giggle. Laughing alone in a public place is never a good sign, especially when wearing mismatched clothes chosen purely for warmth.

She sips the thick chocolate, inhaling its rich scent. The warm kick of the cinnamon reminds her of the Mexican hot chocolate her mother used to make for her after school on grey San Francisco winter afternoons. Closing her eyes, she wishes herself back to those days, when her biggest problem was finishing her flash cards for AP World History. She had always imagined the same comforting afterschool ritual with her own children. That's never going to happen. Bitterness, her old companion, surges through her.

Her stomach shifts and bubbles alarmingly. She sits up straight, her mouth twisting with alarm. Clenching her teeth against her quickly rising gorge, she puts her half-empty mug on the crooked table, heedless of its sloshing, and hurries out of the cafe.

She makes it around the corner of the building before bringing up the hot chocolate, and her breakfast besides, with a sickening splat in the alley's gutter. After a couple more heaves, she leans her forehead against the building's crumbling brick wall; its icy roughness feels like a blessing. Bile burns the back of her throat and her nostrils. She finds an old tissue in another handy pocket and uses it to wipe her mouth. The virus going around the archaeology team has caught up with her. She needs to go home—but that means returning to the sewer for her backpack, and that's the last place she wants to go.

"Julia."

Ted's voice from behind her startles her badly. Why do people keep sneaking up on her? As she turns, her foot slides a bit in the congealing vomit, but Ted reaches out and catches her before she falls. She hugs him hard, even more tightly after her reflex subsides and she's found her balance.

Painfully aware of both her horrid breath and the way they left things the night before, she looks down at her feet and whispers, "What are you doing here?"

"I had to talk to you. I texted you and tried to call a bunch of times, but then I realized that you probably don't get any cell coverage underground. So I had my TA take my class, and I came to find you. Bronwen said she hadn't seen you, but she gave me your stuff." Ted shrugs her backpack off his shoulder and hands it to Julia. "She was too distracted to be of much use—I take it you did what you promised. I figured you hadn't gotten far without your backpack, so I thought I'd look around a bit. Are you all right?" He looks at the mess in the gutter. "What's going on?"

"I don't know." Julia fishes a tin of mints out of the bottom of her bag and pops several of them into her mouth. She crunches them vigorously, letting the sharp wintergreen burn away the tang of vomit. "It's probably the stomach virus Bronwen and Thayne both had. It would probably serve me right for pretending to be sick this week." She looks at Ted, heart thudding. "Why were you so anxious to reach me?"

He reaches out and crushes her in another tight hug. "Because I was wrong, and I couldn't stand not telling you so for one more minute. I'm so sorry," he whispers into her hair. "Please forgive me for doubting you and saying those horrible things. Let's go home. Can I have a do-over?"

"Absolutely," she whispers.

CHAPTER NINE

ack at the flat, Ted reads the translation slowly and carefully this time. He pauses to look up the exact scriptures Julia did, his lips moving as he makes careful notes in his journal. Julia lies on the couch, watching him while sucking on ice cubes. Next Ted examines every digital photo she took of the leaves of the scroll. Even though Julia knows the runes are worse than gibberish to Ted, she's relieved that he's taking her seriously. His whole process drags on forever, but Julia forces herself to be patient. Time telescopes and lengthens when she's sick, and her anticipation of Ted's response makes it even worse. Finally, he sets the laptop on their rickety coffee table and sits back in the armchair.

"Wow," he breathes, staring off into space.

After a few seconds, Julia ventures, "Where 'wow' equates to..."

"It equates to the fact that you're amazing, and I was an even bigger jerk than I thought. It's just so much to take in."

"But you believe me? That it's real?" Julia barely dares to hope.

He smiles weakly. "Yeah, I believe you. But I need to pray about this. Is that okay?"

"Yeah, of course. I don't think I can kneel, though."

"Don't worry about it." Ted kneels by Julia's side and kisses her forehead. Then he clasps one of her hands, takes a deep breath, and begins.

The next morning, Professor Thayne closes the dig and holds a press conference. She calls Julia and invites her to be present with the rest of the team, but she declines.

"I think I caught your stomach bug, and I'm not feeling great," she explains. "I'd rather watch from home."

Later, after celebratory pancakes, she and Ted curl up together on the couch and watch the local public access channel streaming live on the small screen of Julia's laptop.

Alice Thayne sits at a long table in the Kingston Room at the Roman Bath Museum, flanked by Fletcher and an older gentleman.

"Who's that?" Ted asks, pointing.

"No idea. He looks pretty posh."

"Like James Bond crossed with President Uchtdorf."

Julia laughs hard but silently as she shushes Ted. He's right, though. The man's tailored suit, snowy white shirt, and silk tie look like a much more expensive, more British version of what Julia secretly calls the Uniform of the Restoration.

Bronwen, hair tamed and face made up for once, stands somewhat uneasily with a couple of the other graduate students to one side of the seated professors, blinking as cameras flash.

Thayne uses a projector to display digital photographs the team took of the cylinder, explaining her theory about what the artifact is.

Ted talks over Thayne as she goes through the slides. "Wow. Those photos are better than yours."

Julia digs his side with her elbow. "I was using my phone, and I was in a hurry! Besides, they have this super expensive camera and a tripod in the lab. I should hope they're better pictures. Now, ssh!"

Judging from the detail of the photos and Thayne's haggard face, Julia guesses the team worked through the night on this presentation. Thayne clicks to a close-up of the unfurled scroll. The ancient runes stand out in sharp relief against the gleaming metal. She uses a laser pointer and explains.

"Though we are only halfway through our excavation of the main Roman sewer, we believe that yesterday's discovery alone will be worth the time and effort spent on the entire project. This artifact may well be one of the most significant finds ever discovered at Bath, eclipsing even the Beau Street Hoard, discovered in 2008, which was recently purchased by this museum and is now on display."

The flock of reporters bleats in reaction, but Thayne holds up one hand. "I'll take your questions in a few moments, but let me try to anticipate some of them by telling you what we already know. Each page of this book is densely covered with writing in what appears to be the language known today as Brittonic. There is only one other extant example of this written language, which is also in possession of this museum, seen here." Thayne clicks to a photo of the crumbling, tarnished curse tablet Julia saw Monday night.

Was it only Monday night? It seems an eternity ago.

"This badly degraded fragment has only two sentences on it, while this new discovery, which is in pristine condition"—she clicks back to the scroll—"appears to be a lengthy narrative of some sort. A team of linguists from the departments of ancient languages at both Oxford and Cambridge are on their way to study this piece and possibly begin translating it using photographic reproductions of its pages. Simon Worthington, the British Museum's resident Celtic language expert"—Thayne indicates Mr. Posh to her left—"arrived early this morning to inspect the artifact and its contents."

Worthington leans toward the microphone in front of him. "I am cautiously optimistic about this discovery. However, it's important to remember that Brittonic is an extinct language, and any in-depth study and conclusive translation efforts will likely take years."

Ted looks at Julia. "It took you, what, two days? And you've never studied Celtic languages. Why does he think it'll take so long?"

"He's probably being conservative. If I were him, I'd do the same thing: under promise and over deliver. He's right, though. Normally it's nearly impossible to decode an extinct language without something like the Rosetta Stone as a key."

Thayne continues her presentation, giving the dimensions and weight of the scroll then going into great detail describing the perfectly fitting lid of the lead cylinder. “The Romans, of course, were light-years ahead of those who came after them, technologically speaking. Still, the precision of the craftsmanship cannot entirely account for the remarkable preservation of the enclosed scroll.”

Julia squirms a little. Have they found her out? Or do they think it’s a fake? She can’t decide which would be worse.

“Despite centuries of exposure, the case and its contents show almost none of the corrosion one would expect after having been buried in mud and silt for centuries. For this reason, we are attempting to keep our obvious excitement in check. Forgeries tend to turn up in archaeology almost as frequently as the real thing, and we will take extra care authenticating this remarkable piece.

“One last thing,” Thayne continues. “Credit for discovery goes to our intern, Julia Taylor. Had she not noticed it, the artifact likely would have gone on undisturbed for decades, at the very least. We are grateful for her dedication and initiative. Mrs. Taylor could not be with us this morning. Any requests for interviews with her will be handled by our field manager, Bronwen Jones.” Thayne waves at Bronwen, who raises a hand tentatively. Thayne clears her throat. “I’ll now take your questions.”

As reporters jostle to get Thayne’s attention, Ted mutes the computer and looks at his wife.

Julia’s guts are in commotion again. Maybe she was too hasty eating the pancakes, but when she woke up, she was starving. "I never considered that it might be a forgery," she murmurs.

"Why would you? Given where and how you found it, I can't think why that would occur to you. Besides, we both know it's not."

Julia is grateful for his assurance, but suddenly her breakfast is not sitting well at all. Saliva fills her mouth, and she needs to *move*. Scrambling over the back of the couch, she makes it to their cramped bathroom without a second to spare.

Ted has followed her. "Didn't Bronwen say it was a 24-hour virus?"

Julia wipes her mouth and flushes the toilet. "Guess it's hitting me harder." She leans on one arm against the pedestal sink and brushes her teeth while Ted still stands in the doorway. After spitting and rinsing, she looks at him and frowns. His face looks white and drawn. "You don't look all that good, either," she observes. "Do you think you're coming down with it, too? It's not fair, but it's probably inevitable."

He shakes his head and pulls her close, still not speaking, and holds her as if she's made of eggshell. "I'm fine," he whispers. "But...do you...maybe..."

She pulls back so their noses are almost touching. What is he trying to say? "Maybe what?"

"Julia. I think you're pregnant."

year later, Julia frowns at the manuscript on her big, easel-like desk. She's expanding on theories she put forth in her dissertation, tracing the evolution of various dialects of Romansh still spoken in the most remote parts of the Swiss Alps, but she's hit a bit of a roadblock.

Little Jane squirms against Julia's chest in the baby sling, making smacking noises in her sleep. Julia groans as her milk comes down at the sound, but wants to maximize every minute, and will keep working until her daughter wakes up all the way.

Ted is in their bedroom, writing, now working on a biography of the Shelleys. He's once again teaching, this time English literature at an all-boys boarding school in downtown Ilanz. Sometimes on weekends, he makes the ten-hour round trip by train to Geneva for research, though since Jane's birth, he's been increasingly reluctant to leave home.

Julia squints out the big, double-paned picture window of their apartment's living room, watching heavy snow come down. She hears footsteps on the stairs outside, and then the shrill doorbell, which startles Jane. Odd that someone's dropping by during a snowstorm; Julia tries to remember whether today is when her visiting teacher promised to come. Julia rubs the baby's back through the sling's canvas and walks with soothing deep knee bends to the front door.

She opens it and gets a shock; it's not Soeur Malan. Instead, Professor Thayne stands on the stoop, shaking snow out of the fake fur trimming her hood. She looks practically spherical in her long goose-down coat, and when she smiles, it's clear that the professor is still too busy to bother with having her teeth whitened.

"Julia!" the professor crows. "It took me a good bit to track you down! But this is quite the winter wonderland, isn't it? May I come in?"

"Oh! Of course, I'm so sorry." She steps back so Thayne can get by.

Jane is now fully awake, moving her arms and legs while rooting for the food she can sense nearby. Julia stalls with more back rubbing and bouncing. "Please, come in. I'd offer you some tea, but—"

Jane starts to cry.

"I need to feed her first," Julia finishes, a little louder.

Ted comes to the bedroom door, his eyes wary, but his manners take over at once, and he hurries forward to shake Thayne's hand. "What a pleasant surprise, Professor. May I take your coat?"

translate this; therefore, no one else can, either.'" She pauses, looking for a reaction from Thayne.

Tell her everything. That simple, sweet voice again.

Wait—really? Julia silently asks. But the direction is as clear as it's ever been. She glances at Ted, who nods. Wincing inwardly, Julia dives in.

"Professor...I wasn't entirely honest with you and the team regarding the scroll. I actually found it a few days before I showed it to Bronwen." Now that she's finally confessing, the words come faster and faster. "I took it home with me...and I translated it. Then I put it back. I'm sorry. I know I violated your trust, and I'll face the consequences."

Thayne doesn't look angry, or even surprised. "I know what you did."

Shock drops the bottom out of Julia's stomach, and Jane squirms again. Partly to mask confusion, Julia switches the baby to the other side. Now her mouth is like a desert, but she's afraid that getting up for water will look like she's stalling. "How? How long have you known?"

"Since a week after the press conference. I did an analysis of the cylinder's exterior and found the merest trace of blood—which, of course would never have survived being buried in centuries' worth of mud. Imagine my surprise when the DNA analysis showed that it belonged to twenty-first century you. At first, I thought you might have scraped yourself at your station, and the blood had fallen on the artifact. Then, briefly, I wondered if you had forged the whole thing. But tests authenticated the cylinder as from the first century, and then I realized that if you had taken it and opened it, that solved one of our biggest mysteries: We couldn't figure out why it had been so easy to open; it should have been fused shut. And if it had somehow come unsealed over the centuries, why hadn't the contents been damaged?" Thayne is smiling again. "Your taking it and putting it back solved the mystery."

"I see." Julia's face is burning. "Who else knows?"

Leaning back, Thayne gives Julia a long, measured look. "No one. I've kept all of this to myself."

Julia feels intense relief, then puzzlement. "But why?" Something embarrassing occurs to her. "So at the party at the end of the project...you already knew, and you didn't say anything."

The professor shakes her head. "I was shocked and furious at first, but after thinking about it, I didn't feel right about confronting you. It seemed beside the point and entirely unnecessary."

After letting out a shuddering breath, Julia asks, "Okay, well, thank you. But why come to me now?"

Thayne sits forward, her elbows on her knees. "Because, Julia. I was hoping Worthington's work would sit as poorly with you as it does with me. And because I'm fairly certain you've got proof as to why."

Julia looks down at her baby. Her little stomach round and full, Jane has fallen asleep. Julia shifts her until she's on her shoulder, then pats her softly until she belches. Thayne chortles at the sound.

Show her. Like you showed Ted.

"I'll be right back." Julia goes to the nursery, unstraps the sling, and lays it down, baby and all, in the crib. She covers Jane with the knitted coverlet Grandma Taylor made her and looks down at Jane for a few seconds. Their own miracle.

Back in the living room, Julia grabs her laptop from her desk. She sits with their guest again and opens the file of her translation. Silently, she hands the computer to Thayne.

The professor scrolls through the text, as painstakingly as Ted did a year earlier. With a rush of heat that suffuses her and seems to radiate outward, Julia sees Thayne weeping as she reads. Ted kneads Julia's shoulder, his attention on the professor.

Warmth and peace settle over the room, and Julia gazes out the windows. The snow continues to fall as silently as a blessing. Behind the low, heavy clouds, the sun must be setting, because the room gets so dim that the light of the laptop screen makes Thayne's face glow.

Finally, the professor looks up at them, tears funneling down her lined cheeks. Unknowingly, she echoes Julia's own words, whispered in realization at the Davieses' piano so many months before.

"This is it."

Julia nods and grins, feeling like she'll soon float up and off their shabby couch. "I know."

ACKNOWLEDGMENTS

The lovely Tan Morgan first told me about the real-life curse tablets; I owe the germ of this story to her.

The gallant John Messenger, a native son of York, was indispensable as my English reader. If any errors regarding that "green and pleasant land" remain, they are my own.

Robison Wells and Krista Jensen were astute early readers.

Eve Bunting, Susan Goldman Rubin, Martha Tolles, Tony Johnston, and Lael Littke were tireless critics and cheerleaders through week after week of drafting and revision.

Steven Peck, Neylan McBaine, Julie Berry, and Luisa Johnston provided excellent feedback on the final draft.

Finally, this book would not have been written without the help of Annette Lyon and Patrick Perkins.

COLOPHON

Prayers in Bath is the 30th project published by Mormon Artists Group. Its type is set in Chronicle Deck and Calibre. A limited edition of the book was printed on Mohawk Superfine paper with an Epson Artisan 1430 printer and bound by hand by Glen Nelson in an edition of 50 copies. The book was designed by Cameron King, inspired by four original paintings created by Jacqui Larsen for the book that were reproduced and bound into it.

Made in the USA
San Bernardino, CA
30 March 2017